A GEORGIANA ___ MYSTERY

LITTLE SHATTERED DREAMS

CHERYL BRADSHAW

NEW YORK TIMES BESTSELLING AUTHOR

First US edition February 2023

ISBN: 979-8-9881615-5-4

"The ant, who has toiled and dragged a crumb to his nest, will furiously defend the fruit of his labor, against whatever robber assails him."

—Abraham Lincoln

Quinn Abernathy leaned back on the pillow and breathed in the cool night air, flowing through the open patio door. It was the end of day two of a weeklong stay at The Soul Awakens, a retreat known for its classes on mindfulness, wellness, and the overall care of one's soul. The Pismo Beach, California retreat was so popular it had a wait list, and given they only accepted a handful of people at a time, Quinn felt privileged she'd made it at long last.

At fifty-five years old, Quinn had been through her fair share of experiences in life.

Two divorces.

One child.

One failed business.

One successful one.

A nasty bout of breast cancer.

And a heart-wrenching memory she wanted to forget.

So many hopes and dreams.

So many of them shattered.

Life had been chockful of choices, both good and bad.

But the days of living in the past were over.

At present, Quinn was a cancer-free, empty nester in need of direction—something she hoped to find before the week was over. The time had come to shed her past turmoil, to learn to forgive herself, forgive those she felt had wronged her, and to rise above the painful memories that had plagued her for decades.

Tonight's self-discovery assignment was to reminisce on positive memories, and to ponder on what had brought her joy over the years. Quinn recalled the day she'd started college, and the first boy she'd met there. They'd been friends at first, then they became inseparable, always by each other's side. It wasn't until two years later that she realized she loved him. But by then, he'd moved on, becoming engaged to someone else, and it was too late.

Think positive memories, Quinn.

Happy times.

Not sad.

The gentle reminder led her to the happiest of all memories— the day her daughter was born. Nothing compared to being a mother. Well, *almost* nothing.

One week earlier she'd received a call from her daughter and was given some exciting news. Her daughter was pregnant. In seven months, Quinn would become a grandmother for the first time.

Life was looking up.

And Quinn was looking up with it.

A light knock at the door brought her out of her thoughts and into the present moment. She looked out the peephole, smiling when she saw Clara, one of the retreat's attendants, standing on the other side.

Quinn unlocked the door and opened it.

"Here's the chamomile tea you requested," Clara said. "Is there anything else I can bring you?"

"Is it still possible to sit in the hot tub? I'm trying to do tonight's assignment, but it's been a hard day. I'm a bit all over the place with my thoughts."

Clara glanced at her watch and frowned. "I'm sorry. The pool facilities are closed for the evening, though I may have another solution. Karl offers late-night mindfulness consultations from time to time. Would you like me to see if he's available?"

"Oh, no. It's all right. I should get to bed soon anyway."

"Are you sure? It's no problem."

Quinn hesitated a moment, then relented. "Sure. Why not?"

Clara made a quick call, nodded, then another frown.

"He's occupied at the moment," she said. "If you can wait, he can see you as soon as he's free. Will that work for you?"

Given how restless Quinn had been since she arrived at the retreat, she was sure she'd still be awake even if she retired for the night. Plus, she'd had a rough evening. It would be nice to talk to someone about it. "All right. I'll see him."

"Perfect. I'll return to let you know when he's ready for you, and you can meet him in bungalow three."

Quinn offered a quick nod and went to the kitchen. She remained there for a time, sipping on her tea and thinking about what she'd say to Karl. Then she headed to the dresser in her bedroom to change out of her pajamas and into something more appropriate. The curtain over the sliding glass door fluttered in the breeze, catching her eye. The door was a lot more ajar than it had been when she'd first opened it—a lot more. Given the weight of the glass, it didn't seem possible for it to move so much on its own.

She approached the door and peered outside, seeing nothing but an array of twinkling lights around the circular roofs of the bungalows in the distance.

Ah well.

Maybe I opened it more than I thought.

Quinn closed the door and pulled the dresser drawer open. A flicker of movement danced along the wall, a shadow cast by the bedside lamp. She pressed a hand to her chest and gasped.

She was no longer alone.

"Faith, is that you?" she asked.

No response.

"Hello? Who's there?"

In a panic, Quinn scanned the area around the dresser, looking for anything she could use to defend herself if the need arose.

Finding nothing, she swallowed back the fear rising within her and turned around. The intruder had retreated into the bathroom, veiling themselves in the darkness inside.

"Who are you?" Quinn demanded. "What are you doing in my room?"

Silence.

"Whoever you are, you need to get out of here," Quinn said.

Silence.

What do I do now?

Think, Quinn!

Her cell phone was in the living room, a mere five feet away.

Perhaps she could get to it.

Perhaps she could get out.

She bolted into the next room, jerking to a stop when a hand gripped her arm, and she felt cold, hard steel pressed against the back of her head.

"Please," she said. "I don't know who you are or what you want. I haven't seen your face. Let me go, please. Just leave."

"I'm not going anywhere," the intruder said. "Not until you pay for your sins."

2

The clamorous thud of some*one* or some*thing* smacking into the wall adjoining my bungalow to my neighbor's ripped me out of my dream. Prior to it, I swore I heard a noise, a pop, like gunfire. I removed the sleep mask from my eyes and sat up. The book I'd been reading before I'd fallen asleep slid off my chest and folded closed. I grabbed it and set it on the nightstand, eyeing the alarm clock. It was just after nine o'clock, and I was surprised I'd dozed off so early.

For a moment, I did nothing except listen.

Had the thud been part of my dream?

And what about the sound I'd heard?

As much as I wanted to believe it was just a dream, I didn't. My mind was wired to consider the worst possible outcome.

I walked to the door, opened it, and looked in both directions. I saw no one, heard nothing. The last thing I wanted to do was wake my neighbor if she was asleep, but I couldn't help myself. My curiosity got the better of me.

I knocked on 2B's door and waited for the woman occupying the room to answer. I felt something on the bottom of my slipper, and I glanced down, noticing a playing card was stuck to it. I bent down, finding another and another. I wondered where the rest of the deck was hiding.

As I stood there waiting for the door to open, I tried to recall the woman's name. Truth was, I'd always been terrible with names, which is why I carried a notebook in my handbag whenever I was investigating a murder case.

Is it Lynn?

No.

Wynn?

Doesn't seem right either.

When 2B didn't come to the door, I knocked again. Still nothing. I jiggled the handle. It was locked. An alternative idea sprung to mind, and I returned to my room. I pulled the sliding glass door open and stepped onto the back porch.

The crisp February air raised a smattering of goosebumps on my skin, but I pressed on. I looked to my right and noticed 2B's patio door was wide open, which seemed odd given the cool temperature at this time of night. Then again, I was always cold. The woman in 2B had a lot more padding.

I leaned over the railing, cupped a hand to the side of my mouth, and said, "Hey, neighbor, is everything okay in there? I heard a loud noise coming from your room a few minutes ago. Are you all right?"

There was no reply.

I considered minding my own business and retreating to the warmth of my bed, but who was I kidding? Until I had an answer to my burning question, the sound I'd heard would nag me for the rest of the night.

Had she fallen?

Tripped over something?

Worse?

Or perhaps she'd had a bit too much "zen" in her day and had decided to hit the booze. This place was a bit too "tranquility of the mind" for my liking, so the notion made sense.

I needed to know what was up with 2B, and it was easy enough to find out. I swung my leg over the wood railing, hopped onto the grass, and slid over the railing onto 2B's patio.

I pushed the curtain over the door aside and poked my head in. "Excuse me, hello? Sorry to bother you so late. I'm Georgiana Germaine, your next-door neighbor. Just wondering if you're okay?"

When I still didn't receive a response, I started second-guessing myself, knowing if I entered the bedroom and woke the woman from a sound sleep, I'd scare the wits out of her. And yet … I wasn't resolved to leave.

I stepped inside, pulled the door closed behind me, and ran my hand against the wall, feeling for the light switch. I found it, flicked it on, and the bedroom illuminated. I looked around and noticed 2B's bed was unmade, and the top dresser drawer was halfway open. A robe was bunched up on the ground next to a pair of fuzzy pink slippers.

Nothing too out of the ordinary.

In the bathroom every item was in its place, all of her products lined up in a row from shortest to tallest. It seemed strange, given the bedroom hadn't been as tidy. I headed into the living room and noticed the television was on. In the glow of the screen, I saw 2B. She was resting on the couch with her back to me.

"Hey, there," I said. "Didn't you hear me calling out to you just now? I'm your neighbor in 2A."

I walked around to the other side, switched on the lamp, and stared at the wall to my adjoining room. There was a long red smudge that looked like blood. Whatever it was, it was still wet. Resting on the carpet was another playing card.

I turned to face 2B and smacked a hand over my mouth. Her eyes were closed, and she was still, as if frozen in place. Blood seeped from a wound at the back of her head, pooling onto a sofa pillow that had a hole in its center.

I placed two fingers over her carotid artery.
It was then I realized 2B wasn't ignoring me.
She was dead.

3

efore I had the chance to figure out my next move, there was a knock at 2B's door. I stood there a moment, frozen, wondering who it was and why they were stopping by so late. The retreat had a lights-out policy beginning each night at 9 p.m. All guests needed to retire to their rooms by that time unless special permission had been granted.

In my opinion, the policy was ridiculous.

I didn't care if we were at a retreat.

We were grown women.

The day before I'd voiced my thoughts to Grace Ellison, the retreat's founder. She explained a dose of quiet time in the evening, followed by a good night's sleep was the best way to declutter one's mind. Maybe the method worked for her, but *my* mind was a lot different. Shutting it down was no easy feat.

When someone knocked again, I opened the door and saw Clara, one of the staff members. She couldn't have been more than twenty-five and was a tiny slip of a thing. Her long blond hair was twisted into a braid, which cascaded over her shoulder.

Her eyes widened like she was shocked to see me standing in the doorway.

"What are you doing here?" she asked. "Why are you in Quinn's room?"

Unsure of what to say next, I muttered, "I, uhh … I was sleeping and I heard a noise. I came to check on her."

"I just spoke with her here in this room about twenty minutes ago. Where is she?"

"Why are you here past curfew? I thought it was lights-out for everyone at nine o'clock, including staff members."

"Quinn needed something, and she has an appointment."

"With whom?"

"It's not for me to say."

Quinn was alive twenty minutes earlier and now she was dead?

I needed more information.

Before I could query further, Clara poked her head inside and scanned the room, her eyes coming to rest on the deceased.

"Quinn, it's time for your appointment," she said.

"She's, ahh …"

Clara raised a brow. "What's going on with her? Why isn't she answering me?"

I shrugged, and Clara pushed past me, rushing to Quinn's side.

"Wait!" I said. "Don't touch her."

Clara glared at me, confused, and bent down next to Quinn, shaking her like she could jar her awake. "Quinn, it's me, Clara. I came to get you just like I said I would."

In that moment, Clara noticed the hole in the couch pillow and the blood on the wall. She turned back toward Quinn, her eyes coming to rest on the back of her head. "Is that a … is that what it looks like?"

"Depends. What do you think it looks like?"

"A bullet hole."

"I'd say so."

Clara stood, staggering backward. Her eyes bored into mine like *I* was to blame for Quinn's tragic end. She jerked a cell phone out of her pocket and said, "Stay back! Stay away. Don't you dare come near me."

"You've got this all wrong," I said. "I didn't do anything. I'm telling you the truth. If you could give me a moment to explain, I—"

"You didn't *do* anything? Save your lies for the cops. I'm not interested."

She was in shock, and why wouldn't she be?

Clara was as suspicious of me as I was of her, and I didn't blame her.

"Before you make a call, give me a second to explain," I said. "I was asleep in my room, and I heard a noise."

"You said that already. What time?"

I glanced at my watch. "About ten minutes ago."

"What kind of noise?"

"A pop, and then it sounded like something slamming into the wall. After a couple of minutes, I decided to come over and make sure she was all right. I knocked on her door, but she didn't answer."

Clara was shaking, her eyes fixated on the wound at the back of Quinn's head. "How did you get in here if she didn't let you in?"

"It wasn't hard. The sliding glass door was open, and I showed myself in."

"What you mean to say is you trespassed. Right?"

I'd only been at the retreat for two days, and in that time, I'd had a few interactions with Clara. Until now, I'd found her to be an accommodating woman who seemed to have found a job that suited her personality. Now, I was seeing a different side of her, one that was much more aggressive. It gave me pause, leading me to wonder whether her actions were out of concern for Quinn or something more … like a woman with a secret.

"I guess you can say I trespassed, but it was with the best of intentions," I said. "I just wanted to see if she was okay. I had no idea I'd find her like this, and I had no idea she was dead."

"Someone was here tonight, in this room, with Quinn. Look at her. It's obvious she didn't do this to herself."

"I didn't do it to her either."

"I bet that's what all killers say when they're caught."

I was growing weary of the insinuations. "Look, I'm a private investigator who specializes in homicide cases. I came to the retreat with my friends and family because I struggle to unwind. Not that it's any of your business, but it's the truth. Now I'm thinking it was all a mistake. I don't belong here."

"Why should I believe you?"

"I don't care whether you believe me or not. You want to call the police? I'll get Rex Foley on the phone right now."

She moved a hand to her hip. "Who's he?"

"The new chief of police in San Luis Obispo. We've worked a couple of cases together in the past. He'll vouch for me."

"Even if he does, it doesn't mean you're not capable of murder."

If she didn't stop squawking, I *would* be capable of murder.

Hers.

I spread my arms, taking my time as I spun around. "Take a good look at me, Clara. I'm dressed in white. I have no blood on me. No bruises. No defensive wounds. No markings of any kind."

She narrowed her eyes, eyeballing me from top to bottom. "Yeah, well, this kind of thing doesn't happen here. And I don't need your help making a call. I can do it myself."

4

What had started out as a brilliant idea several months earlier was now turning into a nightmare to the millionth degree. To celebrate the one-year anniversary of opening the Case Closed Detective Agency with my sister-in-law, Simone Bonet, and my friend, Lilia Hunter, both former detectives, I'd booked us in for a week-long retreat. I convinced myself it would be nice to get away from it all. I thought I'd be able to let loose, take a break from the hustle and bustle of life, from our recent homicide cases, and go to a place where we could shut out the world in general.

Given what had just happened to Quinn, I was certain nothing about the remainder of our week was going to be relaxing. And not just because a murder had taken place, but because aside from Simone and Hunter, I'd also invited my mother, sister, and Aunt Laura to join us.

The guest accommodations at the retreat were spread out over several acres of rich, tree-lined property. Each bungalow in the guest quarters was a duplex, with one guest staying on the left and one on the right. When I made the bookings, I put my mother in a duplex next to my sister. Hunter was next to Simone. I planned to be next to my Aunt Laura, but when I tried to book it, I was told there were only two shared duplexes left, and I'd just given those to friends and family.

At present, I was standing in Quinn's kitchen, under the surveillance of Clara and a male employee she'd summoned. She'd also called Grace to enlighten her on the night's events. It turned out Grace lived an hour away in Solvang. It would be some time before she arrived back at the resort.

As I braced myself for what was about to come next, I heard a familiar voice on the opposite side of Quinn's door. Chief Foley stepped inside along with Officers Higgins and Decker.

As soon as he saw me, he shook his head, threw his hands in the air, and said, "Of course, you're here. Why wouldn't you be?"

Foley breezed past me and hunched down, inspecting Quinn and the surrounding area. He turned toward me and said, "Nice, ehh, nightgown."

Tonight, I was dressed in a floor-length, 1930s-style negligee with short flutter sleeves and a matching robe. Because Clara was so nervous about my presence in Quinn's room, I'd decided not to return to my room to change.

"Hello to you too Chief Foley," I said.

Calling him *chief* instead of *detective* was something I was still getting used to given Foley had been a detective for the San Luis Obispo Police Department for the past two years. Six months ago, when former police chief Ivan Blackwell was arrested for murder, Foley was named the new chief. Blackwell died in prison a few months later, and I was glad he was dead. The man was one of the worst people I'd ever known.

Foley's eyes darted around the room before coming to rest on Clara and Tyler. As soon as he made eye contact, Clara stepped in front of him and stuck out a hand.

Foley crossed his arms. "What can I do for you, Miss …?"

"My name is Clara."

"Last name?"

"Foster."

"All right, Clara Foster. What can I do for you?"

"I was here tonight, right before Quinn died."

"And?"

"I brought her the tea she'd requested. We talked for a minute, and then I left, but I wasn't gone long."

"Why did you come back so soon?"

I leaned in, anxious for answers myself.

"Quinn was having a difficult night," Clara said. "She asked if she could use the hot tub, but it's closed for the night. She seemed distressed, so I suggested she meet with Karl."

"Who's Karl?"

"He's in charge of our mind, body, and spirit sessions. Yoga, meditation, spiritual guidance … that type of thing. I thought it might help Quinn sleep if she talked to him. Point is, when I returned to tell Quinn he was ready to speak with her, she was dead." Clara turned, aiming a finger in my direction. "And *she* was here."

"Georgiana was here when you arrived?"

Clara nodded. "Yep."

"I see. And why are *you* still here?"

"I've been keeping an eye on her. She tried to tell me she had nothing to do with Quinn's death, but how could she not? We're a gated community with security out front. I already spoke with the guard. Aside from the police, no one has entered, and no one has left during the last hour."

Foley smirked, glancing at me like he found this half-pint's guard-dog efforts amusing.

He may have.

I did not.

"How do you *know* no one else entered the room? Were you standing outside the deceased's door the entire time between visits?"

Clara crossed her arms in front of her. "I mean, no. I wasn't. I wasn't gone for long though. Fifteen, twenty minutes at most."

"Still, you weren't here the *entire* time, so you don't know what happened here tonight. Do you?"

"All I'm saying is—"

Foley raised a hand, stopping her. "That will be all for now, Miss Foster. I have an investigation to focus on. I'll have one of my officers escort you out. I'll follow up with you when time permits. For now, you keep what happened here tonight to yourself. No sense riling everyone up until we know what happened."

Clara tipped her head in my direction and huffed an irritated, "Why aren't you arresting *her*? Don't you care about what I just told you?"

This, Foley did *not* find amusing.

"I don't," he said. "You have no proof. You're making baseless accusations, which, if I'm being honest, makes me wonder why."

"I wonder the same thing," I said. "How long have you known the deceased?"

"Same as you," Clara said. "A couple of days."

"And yet you seem protective of her, almost like there's a personal relationship between the two of you."

"There isn't one."

"Then why do you seem so determined to point the finger before the investigation has even started?" Foley asked. "Seems to me like you know something you're not saying."

Clara went quiet for a moment and then said, "When Quinn first arrived, I could tell she was troubled, looking for answers, a way to restart her life. She didn't deserve to die. Not like this, and not here."

"Is there something you're not telling us?" Foley asked.

"No, why? You don't think I'm involved in this, do you?"

"Never said you were. I don't know what to think yet. What happened to the deceased and why has yet to be discovered."

"I don't know how you could consider me a suspect after everything I just told you."

"You're no different than anyone else," Foley said.

Now that the spotlight was on her and not on me, I bit my lip, trying not to grin when I saw the shocked look on her face. I failed, and she shot me an icy glare.

"How does it feel to be accused of something you didn't do?" I asked. "Doesn't feel good, does it?"

Clara muttered something I couldn't make out before storming out of the room, Officer Decker in tow.

Foley shook his head at me, and then turned to Clara's partner in surveillance crime. The young man sported a man bun and loose, all-white clothing that made him look like he was about to compete in a karate tournament.

"And you, why are you here?" Foley asked.

Man bun shrugged. "I'm here because Clara asked me to be."

It wasn't the full truth. I'd seen him around since I'd arrived. He wasn't just here because Clara asked him to be. He was here because he liked her. It was obvious. Earlier, while we waited for the police to arrive, he kept stealing glances at her when she wasn't looking. I wondered if she was aware of it and if there was something between them.

"What's your name?" Foley asked.

"Tyler O'Dell."

"What's your position here?"

He cleared his throat and said, "I'm the chef."

"Do you have anything to add about what happened here tonight?"

"No, sir. Nothing. I was in bed when it happened."

Foley's eyes shifted from Tyler's face to the red-and-black bead bracelet on his wrist. Over the last several minutes, he hadn't stopped touching it.

"Nice bracelet," Foley said.

Tyler glanced at the bracelet and then covered it with a hand, as if he were embarrassed. "Oh, thanks."

"All right. Well, Tyler, you can go. I'll speak to you again later."

Tyler exited the room, and Foley looked at me, a giant smirk on his face as he said, "I see you're still making new friends wherever you go."

I shrugged. "What can I say? I can't help myself."

"No, I don't believe you can." He crossed the room, returning to the sofa. Gazing down at Quinn, he said, "You know, for all the things Blackwell was wrong about when he was alive—and the list is endless—there was one thing he got right."

"And what would that be?"

"Remember all those times he said murder had a way of finding you? I'm inclined to believe it does."

Silas, the county coroner, bent over Quinn, his long, dirty-blond hair falling over his eyes as he scanned her up and down. He tucked the loose strands of hair behind one ear, pulled a rubber band out of his pocket, and tied his hair back. Then he slipped on a pair of gloves, belting out a loud whistle as he leaned in for a closer look at the gaping wound on the back of her head.

"One and done, from the looks of it," he said. "Bullet entered the back of her head and exited through her right ear. I'd say she died on impact."

"Guessing he used the couch pillow there to muffle the sound," Foley said.

Foley glanced at the pillow and turned toward Officer Higgins. "You find the bullet yet or the casing?"

"Nope. Not so far."

"You might never find them," I said. "If the killer has any sense, he took it all with him."

Silas looked at Quinn, at the red spatter on the wall across the room, and back again. "Guessin' that's blood on the wall. Assuming she died the moment she was shot, she was moved to the sofa afterward. Based on the trajectory of the blood spatter, she was shot closer to the wall."

"I thought the same thing," I said. "Why would the killer bother moving her?"

"Who knows? People do strange things in the heat of the moment." Silas grabbed a gauze pad out of his tool kit and crossed the room. He lifted the camera dangling around his neck and snapped a series of photos. Then he swabbed a bit of the spatter off the wall, placed it in a container, and crouched down. "There's a pool of something here, and it's wet. Carpet's too dark to confirm if it's blood though. Pass me the luminol out of my kit, would ya, Gigi?"

I nodded and took it over.

He sprayed it around. Seconds later, a familiar glow emerged.

We had blood.

Silas took more photos, adding, "Luminol is great, but it would be nice if the glow lasted longer. Thirty seconds isn't long enough."

While Silas continued spraying, Foley pulled me to the side, his pen and notepad in hand. Round two of questioning was about to commence.

"I'm surprised you chose this place for some downtime," he said. "Never took you for a woman who would enjoy spending time at this kind of retreat."

"I'm not. This place is a lot different than I thought it would be."

"In what way?"

"Too many rules, for starters. I didn't know when I booked it."

"You didn't check it out first? You're always so thorough."

"I know. The last case I had, the Ellis family—"

"You mean the last case *we* had," he corrected.

"Right. I checked in with the family to see how they were doing a few months ago. Heidi Ellis had just returned from a weeklong stay at this place. She said it was the most relaxed she'd been in years. She made it sound so amazing, I decided to be spontaneous for a change, and I booked it."

"Sounds like it isn't as described."

"Let's just say the picture I formed in my mind is a lot different than the reality. I thought it would be a fun place to celebrate the anniversary of the detective agency. Now I'm thinking I should have taken us somewhere else—anywhere else."

"Oh, I don't know. Your sister seems to be enjoying herself."

"Does Phoebe know you're here?" I asked.

"Not yet. Spoke to her on the phone earlier, and she said she was headed to bed. Got Officer Decker keeping an eye on things, and I'll stop in to see her once I finish here."

Foley had been dating my sister for almost a year now, something I wasn't too keen on at first. I thought their relationship would get in the way of my work, but so far, it hadn't. As the months passed and their relationship progressed, I saw how happy she was with him, and I eased up on the idea.

And Foley was right about Phoebe enjoying herself here. In the past two years, Phoebe had focused more on self-care. She was a lot more into talking about her feelings than I'd ever be. I thought our days at the retreat would be spent indulging in good food, good wine, and a series of hot stone massages. Instead, activities included sitting together with other retreat guests in a circle where we were prompted to get in touch with ourselves by sharing personal feelings. It was all so … eww.

My past was complicated. Not all of it, but enough of it. For me, some things needed to stay where they were, closed behind compartmentalized doors. This approach allowed me to function instead of focusing on things I'd rather forget.

Foley tapped me on the shoulder. "Hey, you hear what I just said?"

"No, sorry. I was thinking about something else. What were you saying?"

"The victim, Quinn Abernathy … you talk to her at all since you've been here?" Foley asked.

"We never had a one-on-one conversation, but I did learn a little about her life."

He crossed his arms. "Care to share?"

"I got the impression she'd been through plenty of hardships over the years."

"How do you know?"

"In the evenings, everyone at the retreat attends a group session before dinner. We were told it isn't mandatory, but I get the feeling they'd try and round us up if we ditched out on it. After tonight's session, I decided I was done going to them. What are they going to do ... ask me to leave if I don't attend?"

He laughed. "They might. Tell me more about the sessions."

"Each of us has ten minutes to talk about ourselves, our past, what brought us here, things like that. And there's always a theme. Yesterday's theme was learning how to forgive those who have wronged us, and tonight it was learning how to free ourselves from past regret. Karl, the guy who leads the sessions, is always saying things like: 'Every step you've taken in life whether perceived as good or bad, has brought you to where you are today. Embrace it,' and other stuff. He's a piece of work, that guy."

"Do you believe the sessions are helpful to those who attend?"

I raised a brow. "I thought this conversation was about Quinn and figuring out why she was murdered."

"It is. Guess I was just curious to hear your take on it."

"What's *your* take?"

"I happen to believe Karl's right."

Part of me did too, though admitting it seemed harder than it should have been. It was almost like I was going against my nature, even though I'd started leaning into it—to a small degree, at least.

"I've always felt when life is easiest, when it's smooth and calm, we float along with the current," I said. "We don't push ourselves to grow or evolve in those times because life is easy. *Change* isn't at the forefront of our minds. When trials come and life gets messy, we go into survival mode. In that moment, we have a choice. We can dig our own grave and wallow in our despair, or we rise up and claw our way out."

"I'd imagine you claw your way out."

"I do."

"I think this place suits you more than you realize."

"And I think we should keep discussing Quinn," I said with a wink.

"Speaking of Quinn, are there any men at this place?"

"Aside from a few of the employees, no. It's an all-women retreat."

"Seems kinda sexist if you ask me. I wouldn't mind checking into a place like this myself sometime." His face went red, like he'd made the comment before thinking it through first. "Anyway, back to our conversation about the group sessions. What else did Quinn have to say?"

"She talked a little about her life, but every time she got a few sentences in, she'd burst into tears. The first time, she ran out of the session, and I didn't see her for the rest of the night. She didn't even come to dinner."

"And tonight's session?"

"Quinn started to break down again, but this time she stayed. A younger woman sitting next to her put her arm around her, which seemed to help."

"What is the young woman's name?"

"Faith."

"Last name?"

"I don't know. They ask us not to use last names here."

"Makes sense, I guess, based on the personal nature of the conversations y'all are having. Before the floodgates opened, what did Quinn share with the group?"

"She'd been divorced a couple of times. Her second husband took his own life, right after the divorce."

He tapped the pen to his notepad. "Interesting. What else?"

"She had cancer a couple of years ago. Went through chemotherapy. She'd been wearing a long blond wig, but it looked great on her."

"Did she talk about why she was at the retreat?"

"She did. She said she came here to start over and to find a way to forgive the people who had wronged her in the past."

"Did she mention anyone by name?"

I shook my head. "That's another no-no here. We're encouraged to talk about our past, but with some boundaries. In the booklet we're given upon arrival, it states we're not supposed to use names, except for our own first name. It's meant to help respect and preserve the privacy of everyone who comes here."

"Seems like a good idea."

"I guess. I mean, they're fine with us bearing our inner soul so they know everything about us, but mention your last name, and you get a slap on the wrist."

From the other side of the room, Officer Higgins said, "Over here."

Silas got to him first, squinting as he looked at what appeared to be a bullet. He patted Higgins on the shoulder and said, "Good find. Bag and tag, my friend."

"Not to change the subject, but now that you're the chief of police, how's the search for your replacement going?" I asked.

"Slow," Foley answered.

"Maybe you're being too picky."

"And maybe you should have considered my offer to return to the department."

I offered him a snarky smile in response. "Not a chance. I'm sure you'll find a new detective soon."

Out of the *corner* of my eye I saw Officer Decker standing outside Quinn's front door. He'd spread his arms out as far as they could go as if creating a human barricade to keep people out of Quinn's place. He was also talking to someone, but I couldn't see the person or hear the specifics of the conversation.

Decker raised his voice and huffed an irritated, "No ma'am, I'm sorry. It doesn't matter who you are. You can't come in here."

The voice of my mother rang loud and clear as she said, "Well … why ever not? I've been calling and calling my daughter, and she's not picking up. Someone had better tell me where she is and what you all are doing here right this minute. Do you understand? Is my daughter in there? Is she? I want an answer. And don't you even think about lying to me, Thomas Decker. I'm friends with your mother, as you well know."

"Darlene, if you could just calm down and let me escort you back to your room, I'll have your daughter call you to let you know she's—"

"You'll do nothing of the kind. Now get out of my way." My mother stuck her head far enough into the room to look around as she shouted, "Yoo-hoo, Georgiana. It's your mother. Are you in here?"

Foley and I backed into a corner, out of her line of sight and exchanged a worried glance.

"I'm going to have to deal with her," I said. "If she's been calling, I'd guess she's also stopped by my room, and she'll tear this place apart until she finds me."

Foley grinned. "Bet you're second-guessing inviting her along for retreat week now, aren't ya?"

"You're not funny."

"Oh, but I am."

"How do you want me to handle her?" I asked.

"As delicately as you can." He ran a hand across his short, thick hair—hair that I noticed had started thinning in the past year. "Your mother has two modes: regular worked-up, and extra worked-up. And given I'm dating Phoebe, I'd like to stay on her good side. I don't want any problems. Still, we can't just let her stroll right into an active crime scene, now, can we?"

As we stood there, debating what to do next, my mother, who had twice the muscle Decker did, managed to shove him out of the way enough to show herself inside.

She made a beeline toward us, glaring at Foley as she said, "Why in heaven's name are *you* here? Why are there officers milling around this place?"

"I can explain."

Before he could, she looked at me. "I've called you half a dozen times, Georgiana. What are you doing out of your room at this hour?"

I wanted to say: *What are you doing out of yours?*

But I knew better.

Instead, I pointed.

She turned.

She saw Quinn, and she screamed.

And then she collapsed.

Mom, can you hear me?" I asked.

My mother's eyes fluttered open. She looked at me, confused. "Oh, dear. I believe I fainted."

"You did. Are you all right?"

"I think so."

She sat up, her eyes darting around the room … at the blood stains on the wall, the paramedics loading Quinn onto a stretcher, Silas talking to Higgins as he dusted the door for prints.

"What on earth happened here?" my mother asked. "And how did you get caught up in it, Georgiana?"

Foley stepped forward, extending a hand toward my mother, which she seemed reluctant to take but did. He helped her into a standing position and said, "How about we go next door to Georgiana's place, and we can discuss things there?"

She narrowed her eyes, her displeasure on full display. He'd interrupted the conversation she was trying to have with me, and she didn't like it.

"I wasn't addressing *you*, Rex," she said. "I was addressing my daughter. Whatever information you can give me, she can also give me, can she not? If I know my daughter, and I do, she'll be up to speed on the details, same as you."

Foley blushed, raised both hands in front of him, and said, "Sure, Darlene. All I ask is that you take this conversation elsewhere. We need to preserve the integrity of the crime scene."

"I'm well aware. I'm married to a retired chief of police, as you well know. I'd never get in the way of police business. I know how these investigations work and what's expected of me. I'm a responsible citizen, I assure you."

"I'm sure you are."

"Good, it's settled then."

Foley gave me a look as if to say, *What's settled? What is she talking about?*

I resisted the urge to burst out laughing.

Welcome to the family. Enjoy the ride.

"Why don't you ladies go have yourselves a chat?" he suggested. "I'll finish up here."

"Oh, I'd be happy to leave this room and everyone in it," my mother said. "But first, I must know. The dead woman … she *was* murdered. Right?"

He seemed torn about whether to divulge information, so I jumped in. "Yes, Mom. It looks that way."

"When?"

"Sometime tonight. I need you to keep it quiet until the police say otherwise. Okay?"

She snorted a laugh. "*Quiet* … in a place like this? Can't imagine that will last. Everyone's all abuzz. Every corner I turn, I overhear someone's private conversation."

Translated, it meant my mother had spent the last two days engaged in what I called "ear extend." She had a gift for overhearing conversations from several feet away, even when people were whispering.

"Instead of shooing me out the door, you'd be wise to hear what I have to say," she said. "I know things. *Lots* of things."

"Like what?" I asked.

"For starters, Quinn kept a list of names on her cell phone. Seven names. One person for each day she was here."

"One person each day?" I asked. "For what reason?"

"To forgive or to be forgiven."

"I'm not following."

"Each day she was going to pick a person on the list and work on either forgiving them for what they'd done in the past or forgiving herself for what she'd done to them."

"And you know this *how*?"

She moved a hand to her hip and grinned.

She had information we did not, which pleased her.

"If you must know, I was walking by one of the bungalows the first day we arrived," she said. "Karl was inside having a session with one of the guests. I overheard a woman say she'd made a list on her phone of people she wanted to talk about. Each day when they met together for a private session, she hoped to work through her feelings for that particular person."

"The door to Karl's bungalow is always closed during his sessions. How do you know the woman he was meeting with was Quinn? Did you see her?"

"No, siree." My mother lifted a finger. "But you know what they're like. They're not soundproof, to be sure. If someone like you was in a session, Georgiana, I'd bet it would be hard for anyone to overhear the conversation. Quinn was different. And that voice of hers … high-pitched and squeaky. I'd recognize it anywhere."

"Did Quinn say anything else we should know?" I asked.

My mother tapped a finger to the side of her face, thinking. "She also planned to reach out to each person when she left the retreat—to make amends, if possible."

Foley turned toward Higgins, asked if he'd found a cell phone.

Higgins shook his head.

Foley shifted his focus back to my mother and said, "Anything else?"

"There is one more thing. She said she'd been having a lot of anxiety leading up to the retreat. Karl asked her why, and she told him a couple of months ago someone broke into her house. They didn't take anything, they left a message on the bathroom mirror, written in red lipstick: 'I know who you are, and I know what you did.'"

7

I woke before the sun came up to what sounded like someone knocking on a door, but it wasn't mine. Hours earlier, Foley and his team had wrapped up for the night. He'd met with Grace and told her Quinn's death was under investigation, but he didn't want the staff or the guests to know it was being looked at as a homicide—not yet. He made it clear that no one was to be allowed into Quinn's place under any circumstances.

Before leaving, Foley asked me to keep an eye on things and to report back if I saw or heard anything I thought he needed to know. He suggested I continue my stay at the retreat, acting as if nothing happened.

As if *that* was possible.

When the knocking started up again, I walked to my front door and opened it, surprised to see Faith, the young woman who'd been consoling Quinn the night before at our group session, standing in front of Quinn's door. She was dressed in pink-and-black paisley pajamas and sneakers. Locks of her short brown pixie cut stuck out in all directions, giving the impression she'd come here straight from bed.

She jiggled Quinn's door handle and then huffed an irritated sigh.

"Faith? What are you doing here?" I asked. "Why are you on Quinn's doorstep?"

She looked my way, eyeing me with a look of surprise, like she hadn't realized I was standing there. "Oh, hey. I'm sorry. I was trying to be quiet. Did I wake you?"

"I'm a light sleeper. Don't worry about it. Has anyone talked to you yet?"

"About what?"

I took it as a no.

"I just woke up and checked my phone. I had a few missed calls from a number I didn't recognize. Haven't gotten around to listening to the messages yet." She shifted her gaze back to the door and said, "I don't get it. We were supposed to go walking this morning. I called her to see if she was up and ready, and she didn't answer. Now she won't even come to the door. Weird."

Weird was one way to describe last night's events.

"I didn't know you had Quinn's phone number," I said. "I thought the two of you had just met."

Faith blinked at me, bit down on her lip, and I saw something telling in her expression.

They hadn't just met.

They *knew* each other.

"How do you know Quinn?" I asked.

"We weren't going to mention it to anyone, but umm ... no, we didn't just meet. Quinn's my mother."

"Your *mother*? I had no idea."

I bet the missed calls she'd had were from the police department, trying to notify her about Quinn. It was something officers often did in person, but I assumed they didn't know she was at the retreat.

"My mother got a flyer in the mail about this place," Faith said. "They were offering discounts for week-long stays in February. Guess it's a quieter time of year or something. She showed me the flyer and said she would do the retreat if I came with her, so here I am."

"Why didn't you reserve my unit so you could be next to your mother?" I asked.

"I guess when she called and talked to someone about this place, she was told if she wanted to get the most out of her week here, she was better off coming alone."

"The same spiel was given to me."

I just hadn't cared.

"My mother didn't feel like she could be here without any support. I tried convincing her she was stronger than she realized, but I guess I wasn't that convincing. I didn't want her to miss out on the experience, so we decided I'd still come to the retreat, but we'd do our best to have our own experiences. That's why we're not rooming next to each other. We agreed to meet each morning and go for a walk before everyone else was awake. It was supposed to give us the chance to talk about how we were doing. Then we'd go about our day."

It seemed like an unusual arrangement, but maybe it wasn't.

"Does anyone else at the retreat know you're her daughter?" I asked.

Faith shook her head.

"Why the secrecy?" I asked.

She combed her fingers through her hair. "It's not like that. We're not trying to keep secrets. I guess I just thought … you know, like they told her … she'd get the most out of her time here if she did it on her own. Maybe it was a stupid idea. It's just … mothers can be a bit much sometimes, can't they?"

She'd whispered that last part.

"Your idea wasn't stupid," I said. "I'm not rooming next to my mother either."

"I've seen you around, talking with some of the others here. Seems like a bunch of you know each other."

"There's six in our group."

"Whoa. That's a lot."

"Yeah, I didn't know what to expect at a place like this, and now that I've been here a few days, it's nothing like I thought it would be. Let's just say I'm the type of person who doesn't find it easy to relax. On the other hand, I can see where people who are coming here to grow or to move past something may be better off doing it alone, their own way, in their own time."

She nodded. "Well, I hope you enjoy the rest of your time at the retreat. It was nice to meet you. Sorry again for waking you."

Faith seemed like a nice young woman, polite and full of life. I didn't want to be the bearer of bad news, but the truth would be revealed whether I was the one to give it to her or not.

"Faith, about your mom ... I need to tell you—"

"I hope it hasn't been too hard being next to her. She's going through a lot right now. I'm proud of her, you know. Every step she's taken over this last year has been a step in the right direction."

The wall between our places wasn't thin, but it wasn't thick either. The first night, Quinn had cried until I assumed she'd fallen asleep. Last night had been a lot quieter ... until it wasn't.

"Listen, do you want to come inside for a few minutes?" I asked. "I brought my own coffee maker. I can make you a cup."

She considered the offer. "I think I'm going to head around back, see if I can get her attention that way. Who knows? Maybe her alarm didn't go off. It's just ... she's a light sleeper. She would have heard me knocking. Maybe she's in the shower, or maybe she's—"

"Your mother's not in her room. I'm sorry. I should have told you that at the beginning, but I didn't know you were her daughter. Come with me. Let's talk."

The bond we'd started to create crumbled as she eyed me, realizing I'd been withholding information about her mother. "If you knew she wasn't here, why didn't you tell me? Why did you just let me stand here, chatting away?"

"I'm telling you now."

She ran her hands up and down her arms, trying to warm herself up. "Go on, then. I'm listening."

"Please, it's cold out. A cup of coffee will warm you right up."

She cocked her head to one side and crossed her arms, tapping her sneaker to the ground. "I'd like to know where my mother is first."

"It would just be better if you—"

"*No*, it wouldn't. Where is she?"

I didn't just want to blurt it out without any context, so I started from the beginning. "Last night I heard what sounded like something crashing against our adjoining wall. I was concerned, so I knocked on her door. When she didn't answer, I went around back and discovered the sliding glass door to her bedroom was open. I shouted out to her first, and when there still was no answer, I went inside. I found her on the couch in the living room, and she was, well—"

"She was … *what?*"

"I'm so sorry to be the one to tell you this, Faith. Your mother … she's dead."

Faith took several steps back, her head shaking. She began wheezing as she whispered, "No. No. No. No. No. I don't believe it. If she was dead, someone would have told me. I'd know by now."

"I assume the police are looking for the next of kin as we speak. They were here most of the night. They just left a few hours ago. And you said you'd had a few phone calls."

Faith dropped to her knees. "It can't be. She was doing better. I don't understand it. Why would she do this after she'd come so far?"

Faith sat there, her head hung, sobbing. It was then I realized she'd assumed her mother had died a different way than she had, and I had yet to explain the worst of it. I knelt beside her. "I'm so sorry. There's something else you need to know."

"No, there isn't. I know what happened, and if I'm right, it's all my fault. A couple of weeks ago she was going to cancel her reservation. I convinced her to keep it. She wouldn't be here if it wasn't for me. How'd she do it this time? Pills again?"

Pills.

Again.

Quinn must have tried taking her own life at least once in the past.

"It isn't anything like that," I said. "And it wasn't your fault. If you're thinking your mother committed suicide, she didn't. There's nothing to suggest that's what happened, anyway."

Faith glared at me. "What are you talking about? If she didn't kill herself, then how could she be dead?"

"The police asked us not to talk about the investigation, but I'm guessing they didn't know you were here at the retreat. We believe someone else was involved, someone who was in her room last night. Maybe that's why the back door was open. When I found her, she'd been shot. There was a wound at the back of her head."

Faith waved her hands back and forth in front of her. "What, now? Are you saying she was … that someone *killed* her?"

"It looks like it. The police can fill you in on everything. I'm sure they'll want to talk to you as soon as they can."

"My mother was a good person. Why would anyone want to end her life?"

Why, indeed.

As I thought about what to say next, my eyes were drawn to a stain on Faith's pajama pants, a stain that hadn't been there a few minutes before.

I motioned toward the stain, saying, "Are you all right?"

"Of course, I'm not all right. My mother's dead."

"No, I mean, your pants … you're bleeding."

8

Faith pressed both hands over her stomach, uttering a nervous, "Oh, no. My baby."

Shit.

Just when I thought I couldn't feel any worse than I already did. "You're pregnant?" I asked. "How far along?"

"Nine weeks."

"Have you ever spotted before?" I asked.

"Never. I don't know what to do. I'm having … I don't know … cramps, I guess. It hurts. I'm freaking out."

"It's all right. I'm not going anywhere. Let's get you inside and we can figure out what to do next."

I slung my arm around her waist, helping her inside my place. The blood was still coming, and it was more than I thought it should be.

We walked together to the bathroom, and she stepped inside, closing the door behind her.

I leaned against the wall, thinking about what I could do to help her, and then I glanced at the time. "I'm guessing your doctor won't be at work for a few more hours."

"Yeah, the office doesn't open until nine. I think there's an after-hours number, but I don't have it. I'd need to look it up."

"I'll do it. You just try to relax."

Faith gave me the name of her doctor and the name of the office where he worked. Before I made that call, I made another one first.

The phone was answered on the first ring with a groggy, "Morning, honey."

"Aunt Laura, I need you to come to my bungalow right now."

She didn't question or hesitate. "Be right there."

In her younger years, my Aunt Laura had been a nurse. She was one of the smartest people I knew and my go-to person whenever I had a medical question of any kind. If anyone knew what to do right now, it was her.

I called the doctor's office and an after-hours receptionist answered. She wasted no time stating the obvious. The doctor wouldn't be in until nine. She went on to explain he was packed with back-to-back patients all day. In a nonchalant, 'I couldn't give a care less about your situation' attitude, she said she'd give him the message, and he'd call me *if* he got the chance.

I was in no mood for her tepid response.

"You may not care about what's going on here, or for the woman who may be losing her baby right now, but *I* do," I said. "Here's what's going to happen. I'm going to give you my cell phone number. You're going to hang up and call the doctor, and you're going to tell him to call me right away."

"As I explained ma'am, he's slammed all day today. If she needs to be seen sooner, you should take her to the emergency room."

"He has five minutes to call me, or I start calling his cell phone, and I won't stop until he answers."

She laughed. "His personal number isn't listed."

"I'm a private detective. I bet I can find it in under two minutes. Hell, maybe I'll look up where he lives while I'm at it, and I'll drive her straight to his house. How does that sound?"

A short pause and then, "No, don't. What's your number?"

I gave it to her and ended the call just as Aunt Laura arrived. I gave her a quick rundown of the situation and introduced her to Faith.

The doctor returned my call a few minutes later. As it turned out, he was awake, out for a morning jog. I told him Faith had been through a traumatic event this morning that may have caused her to start spotting. Unlike the apathetic receptionist, the doctor had something she didn't have—manners. He thanked me for calling and explained he'd known Faith all her life. He'd even delivered her. He would arrive within the hour.

Aunt Laura stepped out of the bathroom and tipped her head to the side, urging me to follow her onto the back deck.

I did, and as I pulled the door behind me, I said, "Has she calmed down at all?"

"A little."

"How would you say she's doing?" I asked.

"Hard to say."

"Her doctor will be here soon."

"Good."

"Has the bleeding stopped?"

"Not yet, but it is heading in that direction. You were right to call her doctor. It's enough blood to be worrisome."

"Did my mother tell you what happened here last night?" I asked.

Aunt Laura moved a hand to her hip and grinned. "What do *you* think?"

"Does everyone in our group know?"

"I'm guessing so. She told me right after she told your sister."

"With her here, I'm not sure Foley will be able to contain it."

"Well, we'll see. She did say not to bother you about it and not to breathe a word of it to anyone else."

I supposed it was something.

Mom wasn't good at keeping secrets, unless they were her own, and then she became a sealed vault.

"The woman who died last night, her name was Quinn," I said. "I just learned she was Faith's mother."

Aunt Laura pressed a hand to her chest. "Oh goodness. Poor thing. No wonder she's not saying much. How are *you* doing? Your mother said you were the first person to discover what happened to Quinn last night."

I nodded. "It's the last thing I expected to have happen this week. We're all supposed to be relaxing."

"You? Relaxing? You've been in a dour mood since we got here. Not that I blame you."

"They ask too many personal questions," I said. "Everywhere I turn I'm being prompted to express my feelings."

"Oh, I know. They're nosey too. Abby, one of the women in guest services, ratted me out yesterday."

"What do you mean?"

"She found the weed I'd stashed in my drawer. My rum, too. Next thing I know, there's a knock at the door. It was the other guest-services gal, an uptight little thing named Clara."

I rolled my eyes. "We've met. What did she say?"

"She told me I either needed to hand over the weed or flush it. Talked to me like I was a child. Can you believe it? We're in California, for heaven's sake. It's legal."

"Why did they want you to get rid of it?"

"Clara said part of the agreement we signed when we arrived was some nonsense about no drugs, whether legal or not," Aunt Laura explained. "According to her, my mind needs to be free and clear of toxins so I can get in touch with my inner self. I told her I was well acquainted with my inner self, and if they so much as placed a finger on my weed *or* my rum, they'd regret it."

"I'd expect no less from you."

She elbowed me and said, "Besides, I passed by Karl's place last night, and there's no doubt in my mind he was lighting up. I could smell it in the air. If our spiritual guide or whatever he's calling himself can fire one up, so can I. Anyway, enough about me. How are you holding up, kiddo?"

"I'm too tired to even consider how I'm doing right now, and too focused on what happened to Quinn."

"Any theories?"

I shook my head. "I spent several hours discussing it with Foley and Silas last night. If her murder was premeditated, and I'm inclined to believe it was, her killer knew she'd be attending the retreat this week *and* what room she was in. I'm just not sure about the motive. Not yet."

"*Not yet,* huh? Does that mean you plan on investigating her death, or are you going to leave that to the police this time?"

I tried not to laugh, but I couldn't help myself, prompting Aunt Laura to join in and say, "Yep, that's what I thought."

9

aith's doctor was just as concerned as we were when he saw her, but he was pleased to find the bleeding had stopped. Still, he decided it best to drive her to the clinic so he could do a more thorough workup. With Faith in excellent hands, I showered and readied myself for the day.

I hadn't made it out the door when I received a request. Grace, the retreat's founder, called and asked to meet with me. When I arrived at her office, Clara was exiting it. She looked distraught, and it was obvious she'd been crying. She refused to look at me as she passed, making me wonder if she still believed I had something to do with Quinn's death.

Grace stood when she saw me, smiling as she waved me inside. She looked to be in her late fifties and had long, straight, silver hair. Every time I saw her, she was dressed in a flowy pantsuit. Today it was pale blue.

"Good morning, Georgiana," she said. "How are you feeling today?"

Her voice was serene and melodic.

"I'm fine," I said.

"It's okay if you're *not* fine, you know. It's also okay to talk about it. I'm a good listener."

Not even one minute into the conversation, and I was already being offered unsolicited advice.

Terrific.

"I've been around my fair share of death," I said. "And this may sound … well, like I have a few screws loose, and look, I do, but being around death doesn't bother me. It's a lot more comfortable than being at this place for a week."

She crossed one leg over the other, staring at me like she wasn't sure how to take what I'd said. "Why do you feel that way? What about this place has been difficult for you?"

"I'm a private person. I'm not big on sharing my feelings unless it's with someone I trust, and even then, it's not easy."

"You're just the type of person who belongs here, then. There is so much a place like this could offer you if you let it."

"I'm just trying to get through the week."

She leaned forward and laced her hands together on top of the desk. "I was like you once."

"Like me *how*?"

"I didn't enjoy talking about my feelings either. I was raised in a family where none of our conversations were personal in nature. My mom would ask me about my day but pay little attention to my answer. My dad would ask simple questions, such as if my homework was done. Don't get me wrong. I had wonderful parents. They were just the conservative, quiet type. Even when they fell on hard times, they just rolled up their sleeves and acted like everything was fine. I suppose that's the way it was back then. But times have changed. We live in a world where therapy and working on oneself is seen as a positive step in the right direction."

"There are other ways to deal with things," I said.

"You're here. Why not give it a try? Immerse yourself in this experience, see what happens."

"I find it's easier to process most feelings myself."

"Keeping things bottled up is much like a volcano. It's only a matter of time before it explodes."

Explosions.

I'd had a handful of them over my lifetime, and they were almost always tied to one thing—lack of sleep. I'd never considered myself to be an emotional person, not even when I was a kid. Compassionate? Yes. Teary-eyed? No. Whenever I started to feel the waterworks coming on, it almost always meant one thing: I needed rest.

For now, what I wanted most was to steer the conversation away from any topic that centered on me.

"Speaking of explosions, Clara didn't seem happy when she left your office just now," I said.

"Quinn's death brings up an old memory of hers, one she'd prefer to forget."

"I'm guessing you aren't going to share it with me."

"Whatever is said between me and anyone else here, be it staff or guest, remains in this room."

"We're in this room now, so …?"

She wasn't amused at my attempt to be funny.

"Clara didn't *know* Quinn, did she?" I asked.

Grace shook her head. "They'd just met when Quinn arrived here a few days ago."

"Why is she taking her death so hard then?"

"We all have triggers, parts of our past that are easier to forget than to remember. It's my philosophy that the best way to handle triggers is to talk through them with someone else. It's amazing how freeing it can be to relieve yourself of the baggage you've been carrying around for so long."

No matter what I said, I couldn't help but feel the conversation kept circling back to me. "I get the feeling Clara still suspects me of being involved in Quinn's death in some way."

"Oh, she does, but she's not herself right now. She'll come around.

She just needs time. I must confess, I didn't know you owned your own detective agency until last night."

"Who told you?"

"Chief Foley."

I didn't respond at first. At this point, I felt like everything about me was being used as a teaching tool of some kind.

Glancing around her office, I couldn't remember the last time I'd been in a room that was this bright of a white. Everything was pristine, in its place. In the far corner, a large potted plant rested next to a bay window. On the wall shelf, there were several framed photos. One of Grace with her arm around a man I assumed to be her husband. Another with her smiling next to a dog. And a third of two darling young girls, arm in arm.

"Cute girls," I said.

She glanced at the photo and smiled. "Thank you. They are, aren't they? Are you married?"

"I live with someone. What about you?"

"Single … well, if you don't count my two fur babies."

She took out her cell phone, showing me several photos of her dogs.

I pointed at the shelf. "Who's the guy in the photo with you?"

"My brother."

"Have you ever been married?" I asked.

"I have."

"What happened?"

"Let's just say he didn't like it when I started becoming a better version of myself."

Didn't like it … or was it some other reason, like her trying to change him the way she was trying to change me?

"Did you know Faith was Quinn's daughter?" I asked.

"Not at first. I saw them chatting here and there, and though I didn't know how they knew each other, it was clear they did."

We still hadn't gotten to the point, the reason she'd asked me here in the first place. "Why did you want to see me? If it's to convince me to open up while I'm here, there's nothing more to say."

"I just thought since you were already here, I'd offer my two cents."

"Is there anything else you want to discuss?"

Grace reached into her drawer, pulled out an unsealed envelope, and slid it over to me. I opened it, eyeing the stack of hundred-dollar bills inside.

"What is this … a refund?"

"Of course not. It's my hope that you'll change your mind about this place. Maybe not this week, but at some point in the future. When you do, your next stay is on me, free of charge."

"If you're not offering me a refund, what *are* you offering me?"

"A proposition. I'd like to hire you to investigate what happened to Quinn and why. I hope you don't mind. I looked up your initial fee on your website. What I've just given you covers it and then some."

I sat there a moment, taken aback, trying to decide what motivated her to make such a move. Perhaps she was worried about her reputation. The Soul Awakens was a newer establishment, operating for less than three years. Once word started to spread about what happened here, if it wasn't handled the right way, the business would be at risk.

Her offer of me returning in the future was as much for her benefit as she believed it was for mine. If she wanted me to investigate, she knew I'd need to forego the idea of "finding myself" during my stay and get to work doing what I did best.

"Why do you want to hire me?" I asked.

"I'm sure you're aware of how hard it is to get a business off the ground. You're a business owner yourself."

"Some businesses find it more difficult than others. Mine, it seems, has had a steady stream of clients since we opened."

"You're lucky. I couldn't even fill this place during our first year in business. There are other establishments similar to mine, but they don't offer what we do. What they had that I didn't was loyal clientele. I knew it would be slow at first, and that's why I put every cent I had into the retreat. Even then, I thought we were going to have to close our doors, but then something wonderful happened. Our guests started spreading the word about this place. It's helped a lot."

"I'm glad it worked out for you."

"Me too. I'd do anything to protect the retreat's reputation. So please, let me hire you. A little birdie told me you've solved every case you've ever worked on. If anyone can figure out what happened to Quinn and why, I understand it's you."

I wondered if that little birdie was my mother.

"Why not leave it to the police to investigate?" I asked.

"You know how long it could take. Police departments only have so many resources. Quinn's murder could take months to solve, or years, or it may never be solved. To think about the effect that would have on the retreat is worrisome. Who knows? Maybe it would flourish despite what's happened. Either way, it's a risk, one I'd rather not take."

I didn't blame her.

If it was my business, I'd feel the same.

"I appreciate your honesty," I said. "If I agree … if I take this money, there will be conditions."

"I wouldn't expect any less. Name them."

In truth, I'd already decided to investigate Quinn's death. The money Grace was offering was an added bonus. I was sure Simone and Hunter would appreciate it too. I just wasn't sure they'd want to give up their time at the retreat to help me solve Quinn's murder.

Perhaps there was a way they could do both.

"As for my conditions, I've seen a few cameras around this place. I'd like to view all the footage from yesterday to see who was coming and going."

"I turned the recordings over to an Officer Higgins this morning."

It didn't surprise me to learn Foley had already gotten a jump on things.

Grace raised a finger. "The good news is, the footage is always backed up. You're welcome to view it whenever you'd like."

Her cell phone buzzed. She glanced at it, then looked past me and said, "Will you excuse me for a moment?"

She rose from her desk. As the door opened and she exited the room, I looked back, seeing the security guard standing outside the door, three hundred pounds of solid muscle, by the looks of it. They talked for a brief time and then she returned to her desk.

"Everything okay?" I asked.

"I was just speaking with Calvin. He's just confirmed no one came inside the gates yesterday and no one left, except the police and those with the police."

"And you. You don't live on-site."

"Correct."

"Your staff come and go during the week, don't they?"

Grace shook her head. "They all live here. They work in shifts, often assisting each other when needed. They work for three months and then we close for a week so they can have time off. But this is their home, and everything they need is here."

"Why require them to live at the retreat?"

"Sometimes guests require assistance after-hours, and that's why I prefer my staff to remain on the premises."

"Why don't you just rotate staff so you don't have to close at all?" I asked.

"Every person who works here was handpicked by me, and it's hard to find good help nowadays. I'd rather keep them here, keep them happy."

Or maybe she just preferred managing less people.

"Talk to me about the staff members," I said. "How many staff do you employ, and what are their positions?"

"Before I say anything more, I should say, I have a hard time believing anyone from my staff is responsible for what happened to Quinn. Each person I hire is subjected to a full background check."

"No matter what you think of them, if you want me to work this case, I'll need to speak to each staff member. I'll need to speak to the guests too, and before you say anything, I'm aware this place values privacy."

Grace crossed her arms and leaned back in the chair, thinking. "I don't know. Is there any way around it?"

I shook my head. "Not if what you're saying is true. If no one came or went, it means someone here is responsible for what happened to Quinn. I can't do my job without speaking to everyone."

"I suppose you're right. Can we meet in the middle somewhere?"

I thought of a way the "middle" could be met.

I didn't come up with anything.

"What do you have in mind?" I asked.

"I'd like to gather my staff together first to let them know what's happening and why. Any tips on what I should say?"

"Stay a little vague for now, as Foley suggested. Let them know we'll be asking general questions. I want them to be clear I'm not accusing anyone. I'm trying to rule people out."

"All right."

"You still haven't told me how many employees you have and the positions they hold," I said.

"I employ seven staff members, excluding myself. Calvin is security, like I just told you. Then there's Clara, whom you already know, and Abby. They're responsible for housekeeping and guest services."

"What about the guests?"

"We host twelve guests each week. Upon arrival, they're divided up depending on where their accommodations are located. Clara oversees half of the guests, and Abby oversees the other half."

A small part of me considered asking if I could swap Clara for Abby.

I didn't.

"I've talked with Karl a couple of times," I said. "Well, he *tried* to get me to talk during our sessions, anyway. And I met the chef last night."

"Aren't Tyler's creations fabulous? I hired him straight out of culinary school, and he's exceeded all expectations."

Fabulous was a stretch for a person like me who preferred adult-size food portions. I gave him a ten for presentation, but the meal itself was a solid 6.5.

"We've talked about five members of your staff. Who are the other two?" I asked.

"Rebecca and Kelly. They manage the spa." Grace drummed her fingernails on top of the desk. "So, now that we've talked, what do you think? Will you help me get past what's happened here?"

"I need to speak to my coworkers to make sure they're on board before we move forward. It shouldn't take long. I'll get back to you today."

"All right, I look forward to hearing back from you."

"One more question," I said. "Who oversees sending out flyers for this place?"

"What do you mean?"

"This morning, Faith told me her mother had received a flyer about the retreat."

"Impossible. We don't send out flyers. It's like I told you. Almost all our business is word of mouth."

"What about in the beginning when you first opened? Did you send out flyers then?"

She pulled a desk drawer open, removed a stack of flyers, and set them on the desk. "We sent these out at the beginning, and by we … I mean me. But I haven't sent any out for well over a year now. When did Faith say her mother received it?"

"I believe she said it was a couple of months ago. Who has access to your office during the day?"

"Everyone. I lock up at night, but I keep it open during the day."

Interesting.

"So, anyone could have come in and taken these old flyers from your desk drawer," I said.

"I guess so. But it doesn't make any sense."

It made perfect sense to me.

I stood, ready to leave.

Grace had other ideas.

 "One thing before you go."

"What's that?" I asked.

"I spoke to Karl this morning about his sessions with Quinn."

"I thought all sessions were confidential."

"They are, but this is a unique situation, one we've never dealt with before. I'm all for protecting our guests no matter what, but Quinn's not alive anymore, and that changes things."

Maybe.

Still, I had mixed feelings about Karl telling Grace about his private sessions. I'd never said anything to him that couldn't be repeated, but based on my limited interactions with Quinn, something told me she had.

"What did Karl tell you?" I asked.

"Not much, but I did manage to squeeze one little tidbit of information out of him, and I thought I'd pass it along. When Quinn was in her last session, she told Karl she had been having the same recurring nightmare."

"Since when?"

"They started a couple of months ago."

"What was the nightmare about?"

Grace cleared her throat, looked me dead in the eye, and said, "That's the interesting thing … she dreamed she was being murdered."

10

think Foley's right," Hunter said. "Murder does have a way of finding you, whether you're looking for it or not."

Simone clapped a hand over her mouth and cracked up laughing.

I didn't.

I'd once studied the law of attraction, the idea that positive draws positive and negative draws negative. If there was any merit to the concept, it seemed to me each of us got back what we put out into the world. If it came up in conversation and someone asked me whether I believed in the concept or not, I wasn't sure what I'd say. I suppose it would depend on the person querying me. Considering it now … yes, I believed. And based on the comment Hunter had just made, it was disturbing to think that I seemed to attract death.

I discussed the details from last night with Hunter and Simone, gave them what little information I had so far, and asked if they would agree to give up some of their plans at the retreat for the rest of the week, considering the new developments.

I hadn't even finished before Hunter said, "I'm in. If I have to meet with Karl one more time, I might stab myself in the eye."

"Oh, come on. He's not that bad," Simone said. "He said I remind him of Diahann Carroll."

"Who?" Hunter asked.

Simone shook her head disappointed. "Back in the '60s, she was the most successful black woman in Hollywood. Anyway, back to Karl. I've been having a great time with him in my sessions."

Hunter, whose long, reddish hair was in braids, responded with, "*You* are outgoing and chatty, Simone. *You* have no problem talking about yourself or your life or whatever happens to be on your mind at any given moment."

Simone eyed Hunter like she wasn't sure whether to take Hunter's words as a compliment or a criticism or both. Simone leaned back in her chair, crossed one leg over her knee, her shiny black Doc Martens boot bobbing up and down as she said, "I like to talk. So, what?" she said. Then she turned to me. "And, yes, I'm in too. I'd still like to keep my daily sessions with Karl every day though, and maybe keep getting massages too."

"I'm not trying to get either of you to cancel all your plans this week," I said. "Keep them if you want—the massages, the classes with Karl. I was just hoping you'd be willing to do some snooping around during your downtimes."

"What do you have in mind?" Hunter asked.

Hunter was an excellent detective, but not a people person. If snooping around involved even the slightest amount of one-on-one interrogation, her anxiety went through the roof. Knowing this about her, I had a better idea.

"What I want from you, Hunter, can be done from your room, assuming you have your laptop," I said.

She perked up and smiled. "Yep, I have it. How can I help?"

"If what Grace said is true, and no one other than her came or went yesterday, it means one thing: The killer is here, among us, someone we've met, seen, or talked to since our arrival."

Simone rubbed her hands up and down her arms. "Ooh, I have chills."

"Me too," Hunter said.

Simone stood, hovering over the two of us. With her arms splayed, she lowered her voice and said, "Feels like we're inside a murder mystery game, doesn't it? Whodunit, howdunit, whydunit … Could have been your mother, with a sharp pencil, in the dining room. Or your aunt with a vape pen in the pool house. Or maybe Georgiana, it was *you* with a frying pan full of eggs in the wine cellar."

Hunter doubled over, smacking her leg as she snorted a laugh.

I tried to keep a straight face—until I couldn't.

After the hilarity died down, I brought us back to the topic at hand. "Let's be serious."

"You're right," Simone said as she sat back down. "Sorry. Please continue."

"Ruling out the three of us, my mother, my sister, and my aunt, it leaves four other guests aside from Quinn and her daughter, Faith. We'll get to those guests later. I want to focus on the staff first."

"I'll take Karl," Simone said.

"Hang on. Let's go over each employee and what they do here. Then we'll divvy them out."

I faced Hunter. "I will want you to research every staff member. See what you can find out about each one."

"Won't it be difficult without knowing their last names?" Hunter asked.

I grinned and reached for my cell phone. I located what I was looking for and then turned the phone around so she could see what was on the screen.

"While I was meeting with Grace in her office, she stepped out to talk to Calvin, the security guy. I managed to snap this photo of her computer screen before she returned."

"Is this an employee list?" Hunter asked.

"Sure is," I said. "I'll forward it to you."

Hunter nodded, the grin on her face indicating she couldn't wait to dive in.

I shifted my attention to Simone. "I'd like you to talk to Clara first."

"Don't I get a choice? Why her?"

"I'm not sure she'd be willing to talk to me after what happened last night. It seems she sees me as a suspect since she found me in Quinn's room."

"All right," Simone said. "Anyone else?"

"I'd also like you to talk to Rebecca and Kelly, the ladies who work in the spa. I want to know what interactions they had with Quinn, if Quinn came in for any sessions, and if she may have said anything we need to know about."

"On it."

"All of us need to be on the lookout for anyone acting out of the ordinary. If someone is sneaking around or eavesdropping—well, *aside* from my mother, I want to know about it. If someone says something strange, I want to know about it."

Hunter nodded and stood. "What are you going to do in the meantime?"

"I'm going to do the thing I least want to do," I said.

"What's that?"

"I believe I know," Simone said, raising her hand and grinning. "Georgiana's going to go get her Zen on with Karl."

I approached Karl's bungalow, and the front door was closed, which meant there was a good chance he was in a session. When he wasn't, he tended to leave the door open. I found a spot on the grass where I could sit and wait—close, yet far enough away that I couldn't hear any conversations going on inside. Though I had to admit, given the fact the windows were open, I was more than a little tempted to eavesdrop.

For all I knew, Karl could be meeting with the killer, or Karl could be the killer himself. He didn't seem capable of such a thing, but even spiritualists had their breaking points.

After some time passed, I was surprised to see my mother walk out the front door, Karl just behind her in the doorway. She blotted her eyes with a tissue and threw her arms around Karl. They exchanged a few words. He stepped back inside, and she started walking in the direction of her bungalow. She hadn't made it more than a few steps before she jerked her head around, waving and shouting, "Yoo-hoo, Georgiana."

I smiled and headed in her direction.

"How's your day going, Mom?" I asked.

She dabbed her tear-stained eyes a few more times and sighed. "I've just had the most enlightening conversation with Karl. It's like the man sees right through me. I don't believe I could hide a single thing from him even if I tried. He's just so gosh darn good at pulling every thought and emotion right out of this old gal."

"I'm glad to hear it."

I hoped it would be all she had to say on the matter, but when her hand moved to her hip, I knew there was more.

"He had me talking about your father in no time, about feelings I'd buried so long ago, I didn't even know they were still there. I never thought it would be so freeing to get things out in the open. And now I feel as light as a feather, like I could get swept right up with the smallest gust of wind and whisked off to … well, I don't even know where, but you know what I mean."

It was dramatic, but adorable at the same time.

"That's great, Mom."

She narrowed her eyes and leaned in, cupping a hand over her mouth as she whispered, "So … how goes the investigation? Any inside intel you care to share with your mother?"

"Nothing yet."

She gave me a look that said she doubted my answer. "Well, gosh, you're no fun, are ya? It's okay to tell me things, you know? I can keep a secret."

Except she couldn't.

"What are your plans for the rest of the day?" I asked.

"Now don't you go trying to change the subject on me. I know you, and I know what you're like. You're an expert when it comes to keeping your trap shut. You here to see Karl? Maybe he can help you with that."

As if on cue, Karl stepped outside and grinned at me. "Nice to see you, Georgiana. I was hoping you'd stop by today."

"I know this isn't my scheduled time, but if you're available right now, I am too."

He glanced at his watch. "I have plenty of time."

My mother clapped her hands. "I'm proud of you, Georgiana. I know it's not easy for you to open up, but once you do, you'll feel just like I'm feeling. Marvelous!"

She gave me two thumbs up and then walked away, whistling as she went. For a moment, it looked like she might start skipping, but she didn't.

Karl invited me inside, suggesting I sit on one of the pillows on the floor. I chose the black one and plopped down on top of it, crossing my legs in front of me.

"The last time you were here, we talked about your job," he said.

"We did."

In our previous session, I'd told him what I did for a living. I also mentioned my history as a detective for the San Luis Obispo Police Department. Beyond that, I'd said little.

"Speaking of my job, I'm sure Grace told you I'm looking into the death of one of the guests," I said. "I'm assuming you're up to speed on what happened here last night."

"Horrible news. You were the one who was 'first on the scene,' as they say."

I nodded.

"Why don't we take a moment to talk about how you're feeling about that?" he asked.

"It's not necessary. I feel fine. I'll feel even better when I figure out who killed Quinn and why."

He reached his hands toward me, and I leaned back. "What are you doing?"

"Take my hands."

"Why?"

"Let's do an exercise together."

"I'd rather talk about Quinn," I said.

"And I'd rather you engage in the exercise. It's not long. Won't take more than a few minutes. Then you can ask your questions."

It was the first time he'd been somewhat assertive toward me.

I wasn't sure how to take it.

But I did know how to offer a compromise.

"You've been trying to get me to open up since I got here. If I agree to do this short exercise, will you agree to talk to me about Quinn?"

"Take my hands, Georgiana."

"Not until you agree," I said.

There was some hesitation.

He seemed unsure about how to handle me.

I had that effect on people.

"I will agree to this … Whatever amount of time you spend talking about yourself, I will give you the same amount of time to talk about Quinn. Deal?"

He was clever.

Cleverer than I'd realized.

"All right, you have yourself a deal," I said.

I took his hands.

"Close your eyes and breathe with me," he said.

I closed them.

He continued.

"Breathe in and hold the breath there. Holding. Holding. A few seconds longer. Almost there. Good. Now breathe it out."

He repeated the same process a few more times.

After the fourth time, he added, "As you breathe out this time, let the breath relieve you of all that is on your mind, all that's weighing you down. Breathe out the past. Breathe out the present. Breathe out all the toxicity built up within you, the pain and frustration, the struggle. Release it, Georgiana. Release it all, and then bring yourself to this space, this moment, this time, in this room. Right now."

I wanted to stop.

I wanted *him* to stop.

But as I sat there, thinking of my agenda, reminding myself of why I stopped in to see him. I had to admit something to myself. There was something about this exercise, something about the breathing in and breathing out. Something that made me feel … *different*, and as much as I wanted to fight it, I found myself leaning into it.

We sat in silence for a time.

Seconds felt like minutes.

Minutes like hours.

I wouldn't have allowed it to go on so long, except that I knew the longer I sat there, focusing on myself, the longer I'd get to discuss Quinn.

So I sat.

"How do you feel?" he asked.

"Relaxed, I guess."

"Wonderful. I'd like to go a little deeper now and talk about your childhood."

"What about it?"

"Why did you choose to become a detective?"

It seemed like an innocent enough question, even though I wondered why he'd asked it. And yet, for the first time since I'd arrived at the retreat, I found myself wanting to answer.

"To help people," I said.

"Your father was a detective. Tell me more about him."

I wondered how much my mother had already said.

"I'm not sure what to tell you," I said. "Anything you need to know about my father I expect my mother has already told you."

"She may have, but I would like to hear it from you. Her experience is not your experience."

A fair point.

"My father was the best person I've ever known in my life," I said. "I wish he was still here."

"What made your father a great man in your eyes?"

"He was selfless, always helping those who couldn't help themselves. Every murder case he took on, he worked tirelessly until it was solved and the victim's families had closure."

"You said you became a detective to help people. What other reasons led you to this line of work?"

I felt a lump in my throat, expanding and shifting as time passed. The answer to his question, the raw honesty of it all was right there within me, and yet I was hesitant to utter it.

But I did.

"I became a detective because my father was a detective," I said. "Ever since I was a girl the only thing I ever wanted was to be like him."

"Why?"

"It's like I told you before," I said, "he was a great man."

"At what age did you decide you would follow in your father's footsteps?"

With my eyes still closed, memories flooded in. All the times I had woken earlier than everyone else in the family, before the sun ever came up. It was hard to drag myself out of bed, out from under the coziness of my covers. But my father was an early riser. I knew I'd find him in the kitchen reading the morning paper, as he ate a plate of eggs and sipped on a cup of coffee. He never sat for long. Ten minutes, twenty if I was lucky. But it was my time, and what made it even more special is the fact we were alone together. It was just us.

Karl squeezed my hands. "Permit me to ask you one last time, why did you become a detective?"

Before I had the chance to rein myself in, I was spilling my soul to a man I barely knew. "There's something about being a detective that makes me feel bonded to my father, even though he's gone. It keeps the memory of him alive. It reminds me of all the memories I had with him before he died. Memories I'd do anything to preserve.

In some strange way, I feel like I'm carrying a piece of him around with me, a piece of his legacy I'm carrying on, a piece I wouldn't have otherwise.

A single tear ran down my face, and I broke contact with Karl, wiping it away.

This is not happening.
This is not happening.
This is not happening.

Except it was happening, and I couldn't deny it.

12

That wasn't so hard, was it?" Karl asked.

"It wasn't easy," I said.

"How do you feel now?"

"Ready to talk about Quinn."

"And we will, but first I wanted to congratulate you on your breakthrough today. It was a big step, and I do understand it wasn't easy for you."

In an effort to divert the conversation away from me, I said, "How many sessions did you have with Quinn before she died?"

"Two. One the first day, and one the second."

"Grace told me Quinn had been having nightmares about being murdered."

He shook his head, his expression grim. "I gave Grace that information in confidence."

"Why does it matter now? Quinn is dead. If Quinn told you something that can help me figure out why she was murdered, don't you think it would be better to tell me about it?"

"Whether she's alive or dead, it doesn't change the fact that she confided in me. I don't feel right discussing our conversations with you or anyone."

"Keeping someone's confidence is important, but Quinn's daughter deserves to know why her mother was taken from her. Unless you're a licensed therapist, I see no reason why you shouldn't share what you know with me."

Karl looked me in the eye.

He didn't say anything, and he didn't need to—his silence told me everything.

"You are a licensed therapist," I said.

"I am."

"Don't you think the women who come to the retreat deserve to know before they start their sessions with you?"

"I used to be a therapist. I'm not anymore. I don't see what difference it makes."

"I'd say it makes a lot of difference. I'm not sure people would open up to you in the same way if they knew."

Or maybe they would.

I wasn't sure.

"When I look back on those days now, to the man I was before, it seems like another lifetime, a person I no longer recognize. Back then, when I met with clients, there were times when it seemed like I knew what they were going to say before they said it. Once I discovered I was more in tune with people than I realized, I knew the path I was on wasn't the right one. I started attending retreats and seminars so I could learn how to fine-tune and develop the intuition I already had."

To most, his confession would have sounded like a lot of mumbo jumbo, but for years I'd had strange dreams whenever I worked a homicide case, dreams that pointed me in a direction, showing me the way but never giving me the answers.

If what he said was true—if he *knew* things—what did he know about me?

"What has your intuition told you about me?" I asked.

He smiled like he expected the question. "Why do you think I asked more than once about your profession?"

Touché.

"What else do you think you know about me?" I asked.

"I thought you were interested in talking about Quinn."

He was right. Here we were about to talk about what I'd come here to talk about, and I was the one pushing myself back down the rabbit hole.

"You seem genuine in your interest in helping others," I said.

"I am."

"Then why not help me now?"

He laced his fingers together over his lap. "I'll need to think about it."

Back at square one.

"If you won't talk to me about Quinn, there's nothing more for me to say," I said.

I pushed myself off the floor and began to stand. He reached out, placing a hand on my arm. "Wait just a minute. I do want to help you. Can you give me a moment? Please."

I gave him a moment, and then another, and then another.

Life was full of moments like these, but my day was slipping away.

Just when I thought he wouldn't relent, he said, "It's true. Quinn was having nightmares."

"What can you tell me about them?"

"She said the dreams always began with someone hovering over her when she was in her bed at night, and they ended with her murder. But the murder itself wasn't always the same."

"How so?"

"One night she'd be stabbed to death, the next she'd get shot, the next she was strangled, and so on."

"Even though the dreams weren't reality—not when she had them, at least—

did she see who attacked her?"

"She could never see the person's face."

"Any idea why she'd have dreams like that?"

"I believe it was because she'd started addressing the issues from her past, dealing with her demons, the things she wanted to let go of but hadn't yet. That's what brought her here. She told me so herself the first day we met. She was in a place in her life where she was ready to move on. She knew resolving her issues would be a long, difficult path to take, but she was prepared to do it."

"What did Quinn say to you about the warning written in lipstick on the mirror in her bathroom? I believe that may have also brought on her nightmares."

He raised a brow, surprised. "I never told anyone about that. How do you know?"

"It's best I don't say. The walls in these bungalows are thin. They carry sound sometimes. Best to speak with quiet voices in your sessions. You never know who's listening."

I opened the door and poked my head out.

"What are you doing?" he asked.

"Making sure we don't have any eavesdroppers."

When I was sure we didn't, I returned to a seated position. "The lipstick warning referred to a secret Quinn was keeping. Did she say anything about it?"

"Nothing important."

Another dead end.

"What else can you tell me about your visits with her?" I asked.

"Quinn was struggling with guilt over some of her past decisions."

"What kind of decisions?"

"Some of her guilt stemmed from things she'd done, and some related to things that had been done to her. She came to the retreat with a list of names. One person to work through for each day she was here. In doing so, she believed it would help her get past whatever unresolved feelings she had about these people."

Quinn had come to the retreat with an honest desire to shed the past and live a better life, a life that had been stripped away from her the moment she tried to get it back together. It was cruel. But so was life sometimes.

"What past issues did Quinn discuss with you?" I asked.

He pursed his lips. "In the two sessions we had, she talked about her most recent divorce."

"Which was how long ago?"

"She never said, but she did tell me she hadn't dated or been with another man since."

"What did she say about the marriage?"

"It was her second divorce. She filed after finding out her husband was seeing other women. And though she believed he was the reason the relationship deteriorated, she'd matured enough to realize her own part in its demise."

"What's the ex-husband's name?"

Karl leaned over and grabbed a handbag resting on the floor next to a chair. He took out a pad of paper, flipped through a few pages, and said, "His name is Larry. She didn't give a last name. And if you're wondering, he had nothing to do with her death."

"How can you be sure?"

"He's dead. Not sure how long ago he died, but I assume it's been a while now. Hung himself in their garage. Stepdaughter was the one who found him. Horrible, isn't it?"

"Did Quinn know why he took his own life?"

"According to her, it was because she wouldn't take him back after his affair."

One less suspect to interrogate.

"You were busy last night, right before the session you were supposed to have with Quinn. What were you doing?"

"I'd rather not say."

"The police are going to ask you the same question, and they'll want an answer. Why not just tell me now?"

"I was with Abby. It wasn't a session. She just stopped by to tell me about her day. She does that sometimes."

Abby, the other staff member who worked in guest services.

"And what time did you see Quinn yesterday?" I asked.

He referred to the notes he'd taken. "Three o'clock."

"Did you learn anything else during that session?"

He rubbed his hands together, thinking. "Yesterday, as she was leaving, she started talking about another bad experience she'd had in her life. I believe it was the main source of her pain, the one thing she wanted to heal from the most. She wasn't ready to give me all the details. She said she was working up to it, and I thought after another day or two together, it would all come out."

"Did she give you any hints about what the bad experience may have been?"

"She called it the biggest regret of her life, the one thing she wished she could take back more than anything. She'd sought counseling in the past, but it hadn't resolved the issue."

"Huh. I wonder if her daughter would have more information. I assume you've been told she was here at the retreat."

He nodded. "I heard she had a medical issue. I hope she's all right. It is a shame. I feel bad for all she must be going through right now."

"I do too."

I stood and thanked him for his willingness to share personal details about Quinn with me, even when he was reluctant to do so. On my way out, I turned back, realizing there was one last question I'd forgotten to ask.

"You said Quinn was focused on talking to you about one person in her life each day, and you saw her twice. You've already mentioned the ex-husband. Who was the other person she talked to you about?"

"It was Faith, her daughter."

was surprised to learn Faith was one of the seven people on Quinn's list. Upon further questioning, Karl said Quinn had expressed regrets over the way she'd raised her daughter. After Quinn divorced her first husband, Faith's father, Quinn started dealing with bouts of depression, sometimes lasting for weeks. Mental health issues followed. Faith was eight years old at the time.

Fearing she couldn't be the mother her daughter needed, Quinn sent Faith to live with her father. The arrangement was supposed to last only a short period, just long enough for Quinn to feel like herself again.

One year stretched into two.

Then three.

Then five.

At the age of thirteen, Faith returned to live with Quinn, but by then, their relationship was strained. Faith felt abandoned, and why wouldn't she? During the years she lived with her father, both parents had made excuses as to why Faith didn't live with her mother full time. They thought they were protecting Faith, but the older she became, her skepticism grew.

In the end, their excuses no longer worked.

The damage had been done.

Filled with teenage angst, Faith was no longer interested in the real reason she'd lived with her father all those years. She felt confused and betrayed. I didn't blame her.

The years that followed were rough for both mother and daughter. Faith tolerated Quinn, but she remained at arm's length until the twelfth grade—and the day her heart was broken by her high school sweetheart. As she buried herself beneath a mound of covers on her bed, she felt more alone than she ever had before. But this time, a wiser, healthier Quinn was there, ready and willing to offer a steadfast shoulder to cry on. As Faith's broken heart mended, she began to see her mother in a new light. The new light led to a new beginning, and the chance to build a relationship they never had.

As their relationship grew stronger into Faith's adult years, Quinn worked on forgiving herself for what she hadn't been able to offer her in the past. But guilt was the constant pricking of a needle on her skin, always there, always reminding Quinn of her flaws. She'd bared her soul to Karl, hoping he'd suggest a way to rid herself of a past she wanted to forget.

Karl encouraged Quinn to talk to Faith that night, offering her full transparency about the decision she'd made all those years ago. She'd spoken to Faith before but had always held back, never giving her the whole story about what caused her depression. Although hesitant, Quinn agreed to Karl's suggestion. They were to discuss it at her next session—a session that never came to pass.

As I left Karl, questions flooded my mind. Had Quinn talked to Faith as she said she would? And what about the regret Karl spoke of, the one Quinn had above all others? Was it possible her big regret had occurred around the same time Faith was sent to live with her father? If the two coincided, it was possible it could have added to Quinn's already fragile state.

Until I learned more about Quinn's life during that time, I had no way of knowing whether my suspicions had merit. I needed to know more. And that meant talking to Faith.

I placed a call to Faith's doctor. He couldn't give me details but said he was pleased with the additional testing he'd done. He'd released her with a warning to take it easy for a couple of weeks until her next visit.

Faith had given me her number before she'd left that morning, so I tried giving her a call. A man answered the phone on the first ring, his voice almost a whisper as he asked who I was and why I was calling. He said he was Faith's fiancé, and he thanked me for looking after her that morning. I wasn't sure I deserved his thanks. After what happened, I had some guilt of my own, worrying I was to blame for her spotting in the first place.

I asked if it was possible to speak with her and was told she was sleeping. Bummer. I had so many questions about her relationship with her mother. Questions or no, they could wait. She needed time to recover while I explored other leads.

I glanced at my watch. It was almost one in the afternoon. If I wanted lunch before the dining hall closed until dinner, I needed to hurry. I headed that direction, pivoting about halfway when I remembered how cold it always was in there. If I didn't want to freeze, I needed a cardigan.

My phone buzzed. It was a message from my mother, the third she'd sent in the last fifteen minutes. They'd finished eating but decided to hang around and wait for me. I started to reply when I noticed something stuck to my front door. Upon closer inspection, I found a six-inch piece of paper rolled up and wedged between the door handle and the jamb.

Odd.

I reached for it, unrolling it to read a warning in all caps, penned in black ink: *You stay out of my way, and I'll stay out of yours.*

14

You stay out of my way, and I'll stay out of yours.

As far as warnings go, I gave it a three out of ten for creativity and a big fat zero for deterrent value. As I was staring at the handwritten note, I found myself stifling a laugh. Whoever left the message didn't know me. They soon would, and they'd come to realize I'd never been any good at staying out of anyone's way.

Why start now?

The note wasn't just a warning. It was a threat. Not only was I undaunted, I was more resolute than ever to seek out the anonymous writer.

I reached the lunchroom and noticed my clan was just about to head out. My mom shot me a disappointed look, folded her arms, and huffed, "We got tired of waiting for you, dear. You're almost an hour late."

The word *late* made me cringe.

I prided myself on being on time, but sometimes in my line of work, other things took precedence.

"Sorry, I got tied up with something," I said.

Simone and Hunter stood behind my mother, shaking their heads, a gesture meant to let me know my mother's sentiments were not shared with the entire group. And though my mother was irritated with me, she'd had the foresight to have a plate full of food made for me before the lunch service ended.

She shoved the plate wrapped in cellophane in my direction. "Here, I hope you're hungry."

"Thanks, Mom."

"I'm late for my massage. We'll have to catch up later."

"All right."

"You think you can be on time for dinner tonight?"

"I'll do my best."

"See that you do, and just in case you need reminding, it's at six o'clock." She turned toward my sister and my aunt. "Come along, ladies. Time's a-wasting."

My aunt gave my hand a squeeze as she brushed by me, and my sister uttered "sorry" under her breath as they followed my mother out the door.

As soon as they were out of earshot, Hunter began snickering. "Your mom is … I mean, she's like no woman I've ever met."

"Tell me about it," I said.

"Where were you, anyway?" Simone asked.

"Talking to Karl. It went a bit longer than I thought it would. I have a lot to tell you both about the sessions he had with Quinn before she died."

Simone rubbed her hands together. "Ooh, I can't wait. Our place or yours?"

"Mine, but there's something you should know first." I pulled the note out of my pocket and opened it, turning it toward them so they could read it.

"This was waiting for me on my door when I returned to my place a few minutes ago," I said. "I'm being watched, and someone wants me to know it. If you're with me, I'm guessing you're being watched as well."

Simone moved a hand to her hip. "Good. Let him look. Let him take a good, long look at the ladies getting ready to take him down."

15

filled Simone and Hunter in on my visit with Karl and asked them to update me on how they'd spent their morning. Simone had sat down with Rebecca and Kelly, who worked at the spa. She learned Quinn had been in for a treatment on the day she died, right before dinner. That meant she hadn't gone straight from her session to talk to her daughter, as Karl had suggested. Rebecca said Quinn seemed uptight and didn't say much, unlike her visit to the spa the day before when she'd been a chatterbox.

My next assignment for Simone was to go over the security footage that had been recorded the day of Quinn's death. She headed for Grace's office to do just that, and I turned my attention to Hunter. She'd just begun looking into the employees' backgrounds and had discovered something interesting about Calvin, the security guard. He'd served time in jail for battery. A month after his release, he started working at the retreat.

I asked Hunter to continue to investigate the other employees and then to focus on Quinn herself. The mysterious incident in her life, the one that had caused her the most pain, was of particular interest. Maybe if we did enough digging, we'd discover her secret.

As my partners in crime started on their assignments, I made my way to the front of the property, where I found Calvin sitting inside the security room, his feet kicked up over a metal desk. I guessed he was about a decade younger than me, in his mid-thirties.

Calvin had his nose stuck in a book when I approached and seemed too preoccupied to notice me standing there, waiting. I knocked on the plexiglass window and he shot up, startled to see me. I smiled and gave him a slight wave. He snapped the book closed, tossing it onto the cluttered shelf behind him.

He opened the door, looked down at me, and said, "Guests aren't 'posed to wander this far away from the main area. What are you doing down here?"

"I believe you know why I'm here. Grace spoke to you, right?"

"Yeah, she did. I already told her what I know. Guess I just don't understand why you need to talk to me too."

I pointed at the book. "Do you always use a playing card as a bookmark?"

"Sometimes. Why?"

"A few playing cards were found around Quinn's place."

"What about it?"

"Just an observation."

"You sure? Seems like it's more than that."

"Is your playing-card bookmark part of a deck of cards?"

"It was until I lost some of the cards."

"How did you lose them?" I asked.

"I left them sitting on the table on my back deck and went inside to grab a beer. When I came back, a bunch of them had blown away. Found some of them but not all."

"When did this happen?"

"Sunday night."

"*Last* Sunday night, as in three days ago?"

"Yep."

I shifted gears.

"You have a criminal history. I'd like to know more about it."

He narrowed his eyes and blew out a frustrated sigh. "My past has nothing to do with you or what happened here. It don't concern you. There's nothing to say."

There was plenty to say, and I was prepared to stand there as long as needed to get him to talk.

"It may have nothing to do with you," I said. "Or it may have everything to do with you. I'm not here to judge. I'm here to ask questions and to figure out why someone wanted Quinn dead."

"I don't have time for this right now. I'm busy."

I pointed at his book a second time. "Busy reading a book on how to become the next Warren Buffet?"

"What's it to you?"

"I'm not sure if she told you or not, but Grace hired me to investigate Quinn's death. If I tell her you refused to cooperate, I'm guessing it won't go over too well. And a man with your history … well, I'm sure it's not easy to find employment. Not around here."

He shook his head, grunting, "You don't know anything."

"Fill me in, then."

He stared at me.

I stared back.

And thus began our stare-off.

Patience was no virtue of mine, so it wasn't long before I broke. "Are you going to answer my questions?"

"And if I don't?"

"I've cleared my calendar for the rest of the day. We could get this conversation over with now or I could stand here and wait until you're in a chattier mood. Up to you."

He swished a hand through the air. "Yeah right. I know how much you ladies spend to come here and fix yourselves, thinking this place will solve all your problems, even though it won't. Hard for me to believe you'd give up your precious time for a dead woman you didn't know even if you're getting paid to do it."

He was testing me, which was fine.

Unlike most of the other women, I wasn't here for a quick fix. Hell, I wasn't here for a fix at all. I didn't mind being wounded. It suited me.

"I'm going to let you in on a little secret, Calvin," I said. "I had no idea what this place was before I came here. In my mind, it was cheese boards served with endless mimosas while lounging poolside. Imagine my surprise when I learned I was wrong. I have zero interest in talking to people I don't know about things I've spent years sealing behind a door fitted with every lock imaginable. If you're still questioning whether I'd prefer sitting here with you, far away from those compelling me to express my innermost feelings, I would. You can relate, can't you?"

I detected a hint of a smile.

"Maybe," he said.

"I believe you can."

Another pause and then, "I had nothing to do with that woman's death."

"Okay, let's say you didn't. How did you end up in jail?"

"Long story."

I crossed one leg in front of the other and leaned against the door. "I have time."

"Man, you don't let up, do ya?"

"It's not in my nature. Let's hear it."

There were a couple of false starts, like he was working extra hard to get his phrasing right. "All right, so … I used to work as a bouncer in a club. Wasn't the best job, but it paid the bills. One night, a couple of women were headed out, a blond and a brunette. They were both wasted, slurring their words, struggling to stand up straight, that kind of thing. The brunette wanted to hit up another club, so the blond called a cab. When it got there, the blond hopped inside. The brunette turned toward me and said something about me being attractive. I didn't think anything of it until she grabbed my face and tried shoving her tongue in my mouth."

Gross.

"What did you do?" I asked.

"I put my hands up and backed off, thinking it would end there. When I didn't reciprocate, she got angry, started yelling at me about how I'd rejected her. She came at me with her fists, throwing punches in the air, not landing any of them. I kept taking steps back, hoping to fend her off."

"I'm guessing you weren't successful."

"No, siree. She came at me again. This time she dug her long, pointy fingernails into my skin so deep I started to bleed. I didn't know what to do, so I pushed her off me. I thought if I could put some distance between us, I could help her into the cab and send her on her way. It was stupid, or maybe it wasn't. To this day, I still don't know what I should have done. All I know is, my idea backfired."

"What happened?" I asked.

"I must have pushed her too hard because she stumbled over the edge of the sidewalk and fell. She didn't get hurt or anything. Bruised ego is all. She started screaming, hollering that I attacked her, not the other way around."

"I'm guessing there was no security footage to back up your side of the story?"

"Nope."

"What about her friend or the cabbie?"

"That's the thing. Her friend was too busy flirting with the cabbie, so she didn't see how it all went down until it was over. And no one else was outside the club at the time to back me up. When the cops arrived, the cabbie said he wasn't sure what happened. You worked for the police department from what I hear. Who do you think they arrested?"

"I know who they arrested. *You*."

"Damn straight they did. The girl didn't weigh more than a buck and change. They took one look at me and one look at her and decided there was no way she was lying. To make things worse, she had a rich daddy too, and he was hellbent on pressing charges. It's a time in my life I'd rather forget. I served my time. So, yeah … I have my own locks on my own doors, just like you."

Now *I* was the one with nothing to say.

I'd misjudged him, assuming since he'd served time, it meant he wasn't a good person. It was wrong of me. Looking at him now, I could see the pain that remained, and the shame of it all, a man desperate to create a life that wasn't overshadowed by his past.

"I'm sorry," I said.

"For what?"

"Pushing you to talk about the reason you went to jail."

"Why are *you* sorry?"

"I judged you without knowing the facts first."

"Yeah, you and everyone else. Don't matter. I'm used to it."

"It doesn't make it right," I said.

"No, it doesn't. Then again, you don't know me. For all you know, I could be filling your head with nonsense."

"You could, but I believe you're telling the truth."

"Believe what you want. Makes no difference to me."

"It should … make a difference, I mean. I, ahh, I have a habit of getting ahead of myself sometimes. It's something I've been working on."

He grunted a laugh. "Ask me, you got a lot more work to do."

He was right, and I deserved every word of his critique.

"Can we start again?" I asked.

He shrugged. "Maybe. What do you want to know?"

"Where were you at the time Quinn died? And just to be clear, I am not accusing you of anything. I'm asking so I can rule you out."

"You say that now. You may change your mind when I answer the question."

"Try me."

"Last night I had to pee real bad. I didn't leave my post for more than five minutes at most. I thought nothing of it until today when I heard one of the guests was dead."

"Are you saying it's possible someone came in or out of the gates during the time you stepped away?"

He shook his head. "I reviewed the security footage from all angles. It's not possible."

"Are you sure?"

"I've worked here ever since this place opened. I'd bet my life on it. Whatever happened to her, it didn't happen because I'd left my post for a few minutes."

I was curious to know what Simone might have found on the footage, and if it matched Calvin's story.

"Who's here when you're not?" I asked. "I assume you're not here all day and night?"

"You're right. When I'm not here, I get a notification if anyone comes anywhere near the gates. I can communicate through the speaker in the security camera from my room, or anywhere I am for that matter."

"Did you see anything out of the ordinary last night?" I asked.

He took a deep breath in.

There *was* something, something he may not have mentioned yet.

"I should have said this before," he said.

"Should have said what?"

"Quinn almost left here last night."

"What do you mean she *almost* left?"

"A woman showed up here to collect her."

"At what time?" I asked.

"Security footage has her arriving at about eight or so. The woman pulled up to the gate, put her car in park, and stepped out.

I walked over to her. She said she was a friend of Quinn's and was here to pick her up."

"Why?"

"The woman said Quinn felt like it was a mistake to come here, and she didn't want to be here any longer."

"But Quinn didn't leave," I said.

"No, she didn't."

I tapped a finger to the side of my face, thinking. Why would Quinn ask to be picked up, according to this woman, and then not leave as she intended? It made no sense.

While I pondered that question, Calvin continued. "I called up to Quinn's room and told her a woman was here to see her. Next thing I know, Quinn's at the gate, demanding I open it like we were keeping her against her will. Just to be clear, we're not gated to keep people *in*. We're gated to keep people *out*. Guests can come and go whenever they choose, but visitors? Different story."

"Why do you need to keep people out?"

"There was an incident not long after this place opened. A woman came here to get away from an abusive situation at home. A few days in, she called the guy who'd been abusing her and told him where she was and why. He showed up here and started smacking her around. It wasn't good. The next week, Grace hired me, installed a gate, security cameras, and fencing around the property so nothing like that would ever happen again."

"Grace wants the women here to feel safe," I said.

"She does. Now when someone has a visitor, we check in with the guest to make sure they want to see the person who's visiting."

It made sense, and I applauded Grace for her efforts. She wasn't joking in what she'd told me earlier. She had put everything into making this place the ultimate sanctuary.

"Back to Quinn," I said. "What happened after you opened the gate?"

"Quinn got inside the car and talked to the other woman for a while."

"How long?"

"Ten … fifteen minutes. I can get you the exact time if you want."

"I might. What happened after they talked?"

"Quinn got out of the car, waved to the woman, and the woman drove off. When she walked back to the gate, I asked her why she decided to stay. She didn't say much. She just said she'd changed her mind. I don't think she was in the mood to talk, not to me anyway. She looked like she'd been crying."

My curiosity about the mysterious life of Quinn Abernathy continued to grow with each new tidbit I learned. Still, there was so much more I didn't know, things I was sure were the key to solving this case.

"Thanks for talking to me after the way I behaved when we met. You could have blown me off, and you didn't."

"You threatened to tell Grace I wouldn't cooperate."

"I'm not sure *threaten* is the right word."

He wagged a finger at me. "You and me both know you would have done just that if you didn't get your way."

I laughed. "Yeah, well, I still appreciate it."

I pivoted and started walking in the other direction.

"You have a great rest of your day now," he shouted after me.

I glanced over my shoulder and smiled. "I don't suppose you got the name of the woman who came to see Quinn?"

He thought about it for a moment and then his eyes widened. "I asked her name before I called Quinn. I believe she said it was Jane."

16

It was almost dinnertime, and tonight I wouldn't be late. As I walked toward the dining hall, my phone rang. It was Giovanni, the man I'd been in a relationship with for the past two and a half years. Tonight, he was at home, tending to Luka, my Samoyed.

"How is everything going?" I asked.

"We're doing just fine, *cara mia*," he said. "Although one of us is missing you more than usual."

"*One* of you is missing me?"

"All right. I'll admit it. We're both missing you."

I laughed. "I'm missing you too. More than you know."

"How are you enjoying the retreat?"

"Oh, it's great."

"I detect a hint of sarcasm in your answer."

"Aside from the woman next door to me being murdered last night, there's a guy who does one-on-one sessions with us every day. He used to be a licensed therapist. He seems hellbent on getting me to talk about my feelings."

He laughed. "I can't imagine he's getting anywhere with you."

"He's gotten farther than you'd think."

"Tell me more about the woman."

I filled him in on everything that had happened so far. He wasn't surprised to hear I'd wrapped myself up in a new case when I was supposed to be having a relaxing vacation.

"Is there anything I can do on my end?" he asked.

"Simone and Hunter are here with me. We're good."

"Are you sticking around there for now?"

"Until I find out what happened, yes. I thought about coming home and working the investigation from there, but I need to be here. I have a feeling the person responsible for Quinn's death is also here."

"Does everyone know you're working the case?"

"I believe so, and someone isn't too thrilled that I'm poking around."

"What do you mean?"

"A note was left on my door with a warning: if I stay out of their way, they'll stay out of mine."

"I don't like the sound of that."

I knew he wouldn't.

"Don't worry," I said. "I'll be fine."

"Is that a promise?"

"It's a promise."

"I know what a risk taker you are, but you're also smart. Keep your eyes open, look after yourself, and watch your back."

I planned to do just that.

17

slipped my gun inside my evening bag and changed into a black 1930s-era dress. It was made of silk and rayon and had a drapey neckline. It was over the top for a place like this, but I'd been wanting an excuse to wear it for months.

On the way to the dining hall, a rustling in the bushes nearby startled me. I first thought for a moment someone was crouched back there, watching me. But as I neared the bushes, a large black cat came prancing out, staring up at me like I was trespassing on its property.

I breathed a sigh of relief and entered the dining hall ten minutes early, hoping to see my mother and make up for my tardiness at lunch. She could be a pain at times, but I never doubted her love for me, and I supposed I cared more about pleasing her than I liked to admit.

Simone and Hunter were already at the table.

I sat down, and Simone wasted no time jumping right in. "Let's talk all things murder before everyone else gets here."

"All right," I said. "Did you get the chance to go over the surveillance videos?"

"I did."

"And ...?"

"There was a woman who showed up at the front gate. She spoke to Quinn for a while and then left."

"Her name is Jane," I said. "Calvin told me Quinn almost left the retreat last night. What else did you see on the footage?"

"I'm sorry to say, not much."

"Did you review all of it?"

She nodded. "Twice. Thing is, there's no clear footage of the area outside Quinn's place, front or back. It's like a black hole. Hard to see much of anything."

"Anyone lurking around?"

"It was quiet for the most part. The only activity I saw around the time of her death came from Karl's bungalow. Abby walked out of the bungalow, and then right after, Clara walked in. She didn't stay long. A minute or so, and then she left."

"What time did Abby leave Karl's bungalow?"

Simone raised a finger, indicating I should hang on while she pulled a small notebook out of her back pocket. She flipped it open, using her finger to scan down the page of notes she'd taken. "Abby exited just before nine."

And I'd been awakened by the sound of Quinn's body colliding with the wall not long after.

"That's consistent with the story Clara told Detective Foley," I said. "Quinn was supposed to have a late-night session with Karl. When Clara stopped by Quinn's place to let her know Karl was ready for her, Quinn was already dead."

If Clara was the only person seen walking around, it made me wonder if she had something to do with Quinn's murder. She could have stopped by Quinn's place to make sure she was alone, and then circled back minutes later to murder her. And given Clara was responsible for tidying half the guest rooms each day, she would have had keys to all of them. But what would her motive have been? As far as I knew, the two didn't know each other. And yet, Clara's heightened concern for Quinn after finding her dead still nagged at me.

"Simone, did you talk to Clara today?" I asked.

"I tried, believe me. She brushed me off. Twice. I can use a more aggressive approach if you want me to try again."

"Let me talk to her. She may not *want* to have a conversation with me, but I'll find a way to get her talking."

Hunter turned toward me. "I haven't looked into her background yet. I'll see what I can find out about her tonight."

"Perfect."

My sister joined us at the table, and the conversation shifted from Quinn's murder investigation to the dinner menu. The four of us engaged in small talk for a minute, and then my sister said, "How's the investigation going? I'm surprised you're not all talking about it."

I smiled. "We were, right before you got here."

"Don't stop on my account. I want to hear what's going on."

I'm sure she would have liked me to share some intel. But given she was dating Foley, there was a chance what I said to her would be relayed to him. I hadn't made the time to check in with him today like I said I would, and I preferred he heard things from me first.

"I haven't found out much of anything yet," I said.

It was true. I hadn't found anything to point me in the direction of a specific person, but I did have information to share about Quinn and what I'd learned about her backstory. I also needed to tell him about the note left on my door, and then have Hunter or Simone get it over to Silas for analysis.

My sister folded her arms and leaned back, rolling her eyes at me. "I'm not going to run off and call the chief of police just because we're dating, if that's what you're thinking."

"I'm not saying you would. I told him I'd give him a call today, and I haven't yet."

I glanced at the clock on the wall.

It was 6:07.

My mother was never late.

Aunt Laura, yes, but never my mom.

"When's the last time anyone saw Mom?" I asked.

"I was with her about an hour ago," my sister said. "She said she was sweaty and wanted to take a shower before she came to dinner. I came straight here because Aunt Laura said she'd grab her on the way over."

If she was going to grab her, where were they?

I stood, but I didn't even make it to the entrance before Aunt Laura came rushing in—alone.

"Is everything all right?" I asked. "I thought Mom was supposed to be with you."

Aunt Laura shook her head, her voice unsteady as she said, "That's just it. I knocked on her door several times. She's not answering."

18

turned toward everyone at our table and said, "You all sit tight. I'll be right back."

Before anyone had a chance to respond, I'd dashed out the door. When I reached my mother's place, I stuck my hand inside my bag, palming my gun in case I needed it. I used my other hand to pound on the door. "Mom, are you in there? Open the door right now, please."

I waited.

She didn't come.

I put my ear to the door, listening for any indication of movement inside.

I heard nothing.

I jiggled the door handle.

It was locked.

I ran around to the back porch, hoping her sliding glass door might be unlocked. Knowing my mother, it came as no surprise when I discovered it was also locked. I leaned against the glass, staring into the bedroom.

Night was coming fast, and visibility was limited, but she'd left one of her bedside lamps on. It offered just enough light to glance around the room and confirm she wasn't in it. Not the bedroom, anyway.

On my way back to the dining hall, I saw Grace locking up her office for the night. She took one look at my face and said, "What's wrong?"

"It's my mother. She's not answering her door, and she hasn't come to dinner. She's never late for anything. I'm worried."

"What can I do to help?"

"I need a key to her place."

"Sure, no problem. Hold on a second, and I'll get it for you."

Grace disappeared into a backroom and reemerged a couple of minutes later, dangling a key from her finger. "I'd like to come with you if that's okay?"

"If you don't mind, I'd rather be alone."

She hesitated, and then said, "Sure, but please check in with me once you know something."

I agreed and turned, sprinting back toward my mother's place. I unlocked the door and thrust it open, shouting, "Mom, are you in here?"

All was silent, the only sound coming from the familiar hum of the heater as it kicked on. I checked every room and every closet. I even threw back the shower curtain in the bathroom.

She wasn't here.

I returned to the dining hall, poking my head in just long enough to see she still wasn't at the table. They all looked worried, and I decided not to concern them further until I'd found her.

I checked the parking lot next. Her car was still sitting in the same spot it had been in since we arrived on Monday. I called Harvey, my stepdad, asking him if he'd heard from her. He confirmed they hadn't been in touch for several hours.

I ended the call and ran toward the front of the property. Calvin saw me coming and stepped outside. "Back so soon?"

I hunched over, placing my hands on my knees as I tried to catch my breath. "It's my mother. I can't find her anywhere."

"Where have you looked?"

"The dining hall and her room."

"Could she be at the spa or in a session with Karl?"

I shook my head. "She gave me a specific time to meet up for dinner, and when my mother sets a time for something, she's never late."

"Hmm, that *is* strange. Well, she's gotta be around here somewhere. I would have seen her if she left. Tell you what, let me give Grace a call so she knows I'm stepping out for a few minutes, and I'll help you find her."

He made the call, and we headed toward an open section of the property. It was lined with multiple flower gardens and walking paths. I wanted to believe I'd find her, safe and sound, and we'd have a good laugh as she said she'd lost track of time, but I knew it wasn't true.

She *never* lost track of time.

A few minutes into our search, Calvin placed a hand over his eyes, shading them as he gazed into the distance. "Hey, I think I see something."

I peered in the direction of where he was pointing and saw what looked like the back of the red jacket she'd been wearing earlier at lunch. Heart thumping, I took off, dropping to my knees when I reached her. She was sprawled out on the ground, face down. I wasn't sure whether she'd passed out or fallen or what. Her eyes were closed, and she wasn't moving.

Calvin knelt beside me. "Is she breathing?"

I glanced over at him, panicking as I said, "I ... I don't know."

19

I reached out, trying to settle my nerves as I placed two fingers to the side of my mother's neck. A sigh of relief came soon after.

"She's breathing," I said.

Calvin nodded and dialed 911.

Then he called Grace.

I scooped my mother into my arms, trying to steady my voice as I said, "Mom, I'm here. Wake up. Please."

I felt a tap on my shoulder, and I turned toward Calvin.

"Hey, umm … Georgiana?"

"Yeah?"

"Your, umm … your hand."

I'd been so caught up in the moment, I'd failed to notice what appeared to be blood on one of my hands, the hand I'd used to cradle her head. I pulled my hand back and examined the back of her head, identifying the wound I hadn't noticed before. It was about the size of a quarter—not large—but large enough. I wasn't sure how she'd acquired the wound, or when, but it wasn't deep, and it wasn't from a bullet.

"Do you think she tripped and fell, hitting her head on something when she landed?" Calvin asked.

If she had, I would have expected to see bruises on her face.

There were none.

Maybe they just weren't visible yet.

"I suppose it's a possibility," I said. "I think it's an even bigger possibility that there's another explanation for what happened."

My mother's eyes fluttered open, and she stared up at me. She seemed shocked to find me holding her.

"Georgiana? What happened? Why are you here? What's going on?"

"Why are *you* here, Mom?" I asked.

She was silent for a time, as if trying to recall how she got here. "Well, let me see now. I took a shower and got dressed for dinner. I had about twenty minutes or so before Laura was due to meet up with me, so I decided I'd take a short walk. I never planned on being gone long. Ten minutes or so."

"Then what happened?"

"I ... I don't know. I was walking, and I ... well, it was the strangest thing. I heard footsteps behind me. I was sure someone else was there, on the same path I was on. But when I looked around, I didn't see anyone. I turned back around and kept walking. A minute or two later, I heard the sound again."

"Did you see anyone?"

"No one. It was just odd, so I decided it was best to head back to my room. I hadn't turned around before something hard struck me on the back of the head. And then I ... well, I must have blacked out, and now you're here."

I glanced at my watch. It was 6:45, about an hour after my mom said she'd left to take a walk. I was sure something sinister was to blame for what had happened to her. In my mind, there was no other explanation unless a rock or some other hard object had fallen from the sky or from one of the trees, knocking her out. The odds of that? Slim.

And there were no security cameras where we were.

As if reading my mind, Calvin started searching the grounds, looking for anything solid enough to inflict the kind of injury she'd sustained.

My mother attempted to stand. "We should get to dinner while we still can."

"What? No. You're not going anywhere. You have a gash on your head. It needs to be looked at."

She pressed a hand to the back of her head and then brought the hand in front of her face. "It's just a little blood, dear. I feel fine."

"I don't think you understand what's going on here," I said. "I don't think what happened to you was an accident. I think someone hurt you on purpose."

She swished a hand through the air. "Hurt *me*? Why would someone do a thing like that in broad daylight when they know an investigation is taking place? I'm sure there's a logical explanation. Just because Quinn is dead doesn't mean someone's out to get all of us."

Unbelievable.

"You're not going anywhere until the paramedics look you over," I said.

"Oh, come on now. It's just a little blood. It's not a big deal. I'll just bet a branch fell and hit me on the head. That's your culprit."

"But you thought someone was behind you on the pathway."

"Well, yes, but no one was there when I looked."

"You can't be sure no one was here. They could have been hiding."

"Hiding? Where? I have perfect vision. No one else was here."

I realized there was no point debating with her, so I took my phone, snapped a photo of the back of her head, and spun her around.

"What on earth are you doing?" she asked.

I showed her the photo. "Does *this* look like a tree branch fell from the sky and hit you?"

She leaned in to get a closer look. "Oh, my. It's bigger than I imagined, but not by much. I'll get your Aunt Laura to slap a little alcohol on it and a bandage, and I'll be right as rain."

"This is serious, Mom. You could have been killed."

"But I wasn't. If someone wanted me dead, they would have done more than leave me with a little bump on the head. Quinn was shot. I wasn't. I don't see how the two are related. Please stop making it more than it needs to be."

It was like someone had removed my mother from her body, replacing Nervous Nellie with Chill Jill. It didn't make sense, and the more I stared at her, the more I could see it in her expression. She *was* worried. She just didn't want to admit it in front of me.

As I stood there, trying to piece it all together, my mother started walking away. "I don't know about you two, but I'm starving."

"Mom, wait," I said.

"Join me if you like, or don't. Either way, toodaloo."

Toodaloo?

I don't think so.

Calvin and I exchanged glances, and then we sped up to her. After what happened, I wasn't letting her out of my sight.

"Sure is chilly out here," my mother said. "Guess I should have brought a warmer jacket."

She stuck her hands into her pockets and made a weird face.

"What is it?" I asked.

"It's nothing."

"*Mom?*"

"Oh, all right. Feels like something's in my pocket, and I emptied them before I left my place."

She pulled a folded piece of paper out of the right pocket and looked at it.

"It, uhh … has your name on it, Georgiana."

Of course it did.

I held out my hand and she gave it to me. Calvin and my mother leaned in, eyeing the paper as I opened it. The message inside was brief, a mere three words: *I warned you.*

20

The paramedics arrived and checked my mother over. Turned out the injury she'd sustained wasn't as bad as it looked, which was a relief. While they examined her, I called Foley. Turned out he'd already received a call from Phoebe and was on his way. About ten minutes later, he arrived, and we left my mom's place and headed over to mine so we could speak in private.

He wasted no time. "Why did you wait so long to update me on all that's happened today?"

"I planned to call you after dinner to talk about it, I swear. Then my mother went missing … and, well, you know what happened after that."

"And you're *sure* she was assaulted?"

I pulled out the note that had been tucked into her jacket pocket and handed it to him. "This confirms it."

He unfolded the paper and said, "How so?"

"First, I get a note on my door today with a warning that says: *You stay out of my way, and I'll stay out of yours.* Then my mother gets whacked from behind and finds a second note in her jacket pocket. Somebody here, someone on the property right now is our murderer."

"You may be right." He tugged on his chin, pacing back and forth, thinking. "Start with this morning and take me through today's events."

I told him about Quinn's daughter, Faith, and what we'd talked about before she was whisked off the property by her doctor. We also talked about my conversation with Karl. And then I mentioned Jane, the woman Calvin said had driven to the retreat to pick up Quinn the day before.

After I'd finished, he said, "Seems like Quinn was dealing with a lot of demons."

"I believe she was here to work through them, leave the past in the past, that kind of thing."

"How's her daughter doing?"

"Faith's good, as far as I know," I said. "I tried calling earlier, and her fiancé said she was sleeping. Figured I'd try her again tomorrow, see if she knows who Jane is and try and get a last name. I have so many questions for her."

"Such as?"

"She was the one who found her stepdad after he killed himself. I want to know more about it, and the circumstances surrounding his death. A couple of weeks before coming to the retreat, someone left a warning message in Quinn's bathroom. Did Faith know about it? Quinn talked to Karl about her rocky relationship with her daughter, and he encouraged her to make amends last night. Did she? And did Faith know Quinn was thinking of leaving the retreat?"

He rubbed a hand along his jawline, pulled his cell phone from his pocket, and said, "Let's find out."

Foley made the call, but Faith didn't answer.

He left a message, hung up, and then turned toward me. "Tell you what ... I'll stop over at Faith's place in the morning. Then I'll head over here to question everyone who's stepped foot on the property this week. We need to encourage everyone to stay put. Are you still good to remain here, keeping an eye on things?"

"After what happened to my mother, I'm not going anywhere."

"I expected you'd say that. Since you have a target on your back, it's best your mother, your aunt, and Phoebe leave here. You can't have eyes on them all the time, and I don't want another call like the one I got tonight. Phoebe's shaken up. She shouldn't be here."

He was worried about her. I could tell. And he was right. Someone wanted me to know they'd go to any lengths to stop me from finding out the truth, and they'd used my family to try and force me into backing down. They'd all be safer if they returned home. I wouldn't be able to concentrate the way I needed to if they remained.

"I'll have a talk with my family as soon as we're finished," I said.

"Try your best to convince them. If they refuse to leave, I'll step in. I want all three of them to leave this place tonight. I'll follow behind, make sure they get home okay. Your stepdad can keep an eye on them while we're figuring things out."

"Good idea."

"Did you … eh, bring anything with you … you know, for protection?"

I opened my handbag, and he peered inside. I then pulled up the bottom of my dress, showing him the pistol strapped to my leg. "You know as well as I do that it's easy to make enemies in our line of work. I don't go anywhere unarmed these days. Simone doesn't either."

"And Hunter?"

Hunter had been on my mind all evening. She didn't handle this type of thing well. "I need to talk with her. I'm thinking she shouldn't stay either. She can do what she does for me from home."

"You, ehh … spend much time with her outside of work?"

It was a strange question, one that carried more meaning than he was letting on.

"Sometimes," I said. "Why?"

"I ran into her a couple of weeks ago. She was at a café, having dinner with another woman. Think she said her name was Rochelle."

"Yeah, Rochelle moved in with Hunter a few months ago. She rides around town on a vintage Harley. From what I know about her, she's the opposite of Hunter in every way, but so far, Hunter seems happy to have a new roommate."

"New roommate, huh?" He shot me a wink. "You sure that's all she is to her?"

"You know Hunter. She's the type of nut that doesn't want to be cracked. She's not the oversharing type. I figure if she wants me to know something about her life, she'll tell me when she's ready."

Or not.

I never knew when it came to her.

My door blew open, and in came my mother, followed close behind by Phoebe and Aunt Laura. She looked at me and then at Foley and then crossed her arms as she said, "So ... what are we going to do about the person who wrote that note?"

21

"We aren't going to do anything," Foley said. "I've been talking it over with Georgiana, and we've agreed that you, Laura, and Phoebe are better off going home tonight."

In the time Foley had been dating Phoebe, he'd learned a few things about how my mother operated, but given the comment he'd just made, it was clear he had a lot more to learn. Talking to her in this manner wasn't the way to achieve his desired endgame.

"Excuse me," my mother said. "I'll make up my own mind, thank you."

Foley raised a hand in front of him. "I'm not trying to tell you what to do, Darlene. I'm trying to keep you safe. I'm trying to keep you *all* safe."

"And you think you'll do that by leaving my daughter here and sending the rest of us away? Who's going to be here for her?"

"I can take care of myself, Mom," I said.

"She's right," Foley said. "Georgiana is one of the toughest women I've ever met. Hell, she may even be tougher than me at times."

More like all the time.

"I don't care," my mother said. "I say we all stay, find this psycho together."

Aunt Laura, who was gifted at exercising a great deal of patience when it came to my mother, decided now was one of those times she needed to speak her mind. "Foley's right. We should go. Georgiana *can* take care of herself. If we stay here, she's going to be focused on what *we're* all doing. She needs to focus on the investigation and bring some closure to Quinn's daughter and unborn grandchild. And don't you try to say otherwise. You know I'm right, Darlene."

My mother plopped down on the sofa, burying her head in her hands. "I just don't know. I don't like this … I don't like it at all."

Phoebe sat beside her, putting her arm around our mother's shoulder. "I agree with Aunt Laura, Mom. The faster we get out of here, the faster Gigi can do her job, and the faster life returns to normal."

My mother sat back, eyeing each of us in turn. For a moment I thought I needed to brace myself for round two, and then, but she threw her hands up and said, "Oh, all right. I may be outvoted, but just know I'm not happy about this decision, and I expect you to check in, Georgiana. Let us all know what's going on, mmkay?"

She'd said it out of concern, but also because for all her talk about avoiding drama, she always seemed to find herself in the middle of it.

"I'll check in," I said.

"Is Hunter or Simone staying too?" my mother asked.

As if on cue, Simone did a knock-and-walk, rapping on my door a few times before showing herself inside without invitation. She rounded the corner and said, "I don't know what you're all talking about, but I caught the tail end. I'm not leaving. If Georgiana stays, I stay."

22

As my family packed their things, I stopped by to check in on Hunter. As soon as she opened the door, I could tell everything wasn't all right. I also noticed she'd packed a few bags.

"I wanted to stop by," I said. "I haven't seen you since dinner."

"I was just going to call you. After what happened to your mom, I … uhh, I needed some time to myself. I have to admit, I'm becoming more and more uncomfortable here. I bet you're thinking I'm being lame, and you're right. You're here, and Simone's here, and this is what we do. We take out the bad guys. It's just … I can't …"

I threw my arms around her and pulled her in close. "It's not lame. When we started the business, we agreed to keep you in the background, working behind the scenes, where you're comfortable. After Quinn was murdered, I should have checked in with you to see if you were okay to stick around. I'm sorry."

"Don't be. You've been busy doing your job. It's what you should be doing. I just got off the phone with Rochelle. I thought she'd think I was crazy for dumping all my feelings on her about what's going on here, but she was great. I'm feeling a lot better now."

"How are things going with Rochelle? You haven't talked about her much since she moved in."

Hunter tucked a lock of hair behind her ear and grinned. "Everything is great. I should have gotten a roommate sooner. I have no idea why I waited so long."

Indeed.

I gestured toward the bags on the bed. "Looks like you're heading out. I don't blame you. I was coming here to suggest you leave with my family tonight."

"They're leaving?"

"My mother, sister, and Aunt Laura are all headed home. Simone and I will stay. If you'd like to leave with them, Foley will make sure you get home safe."

"I appreciate that, but Rochelle's already on her way."

"Oh, okay."

"And just so you know, I want to keep doing what I've been doing on the investigation. I just don't want to do it here, this close to the … well, you know … the killer. I haven't been able to find out much more about Quinn yet, but I've been looking into the employees like you asked. I discovered they all have something in common."

My interest was piqued.

"What is it?" I asked.

"Ready for this? They've all served time."

"You mean jail time? All of them?"

"Yep."

"For what?" I asked.

Hunter walked to the desk and grabbed a notebook off the top of it. "Everything is in here. I'll leave it with you so you can go through my findings in more detail."

"Have any of them committed murder?"

She shook her head.

"I know about Calvin," I said. "He shared a bit of his past with me. He served time for battery, right? Well, alleged battery."

"Yeah."

"What about the others?"

"Clara, the woman who found you in Quinn's room last night, was caught stealing. Tyler, the chef, was charged with possession. Marijuana, you know … before it was legal in this state. The spa sisters were charged with arson."

"Arson? Wow."

"After Rebecca lost her house in her divorce, they lit it on fire. No one was in the home at the time."

"What about the other employee in guest services, Abby?"

"Abby got into a bar fight. The girl she sparred with ended up in the hospital with several broken bones."

"When were they released from jail?" I asked.

"All within the last four years."

I sat on Hunter's bed, crossing one leg over the other as I flipped through Hunter's notes, processing everything she'd just said. It seemed Grace liked hiring people who'd been through tough times in their lives, times when they were down on their luck. I had to admit, it fit with her philosophy about helping others to become better versions of themselves.

Grace was a fixer.

Even so, I wasn't so sure bringing them to a place like this was the right move. If Calvin's version of things was true, and I believed it was, his crime could be chocked up to a simple misunderstanding. As for Tyler, marijuana possession wasn't an offense anymore. And Clara could have become a thief for several different reasons.

The other three, the ones I'd take a closer look at, had all lashed out in anger. Rebecca and Kelly in an anger-fueled moment had torched a house. And then there was Abby, who'd lost control of her emotions at a bar.

Tomorrow was going to be an eye-opener.

Hunter's phone buzzed.

She pulled up a text message, read it, and said, "Rochelle's here."

"Great, I'll help you with your bags."

We grabbed her suitcases and headed out the door.

"Tonight, when I get home, I'll see what I can find out about the four other guests, and I'll do a deeper dive on Quinn," Hunter said. "You should have something from me by morning."

"It's late, and you've been through a lot today. It can wait until tomorrow."

"I don't want to wait. I want you to catch this guy. The sooner the better."

This guy.

Or ... this *girl.*

23

'd just stepped out of the shower and was changing into my pajamas when I heard what sounded like someone twisting the handle of my front door. I grabbed my gun off the counter and walked to the door, poised and ready to fire.

"I'm armed," I said. "Back away from the door."

"I'm armed too," came the swift reply. "And I'm not going anywhere."

I lowered my weapon and swung the door open, staring at a smiling Simone. She was dressed in a Nirvana sweatshirt, black-and-white plaid pajama bottoms, and Doc Martens. Quite the look.

She glanced at my ensemble and laughed. "Of course, you're dressed like you're headed out to a 1930s lingerie party. Why wouldn't you be?"

"What are you doing here?"

She came inside, slipping her duffel bag off her shoulder and sliding it onto the bed.

I sat on the bed and squinted up at her. "What's going on?"

"Scooch over."

I scooched over.

She sat down.

"I'm serious," I said. "What are you doing?"

"From here on out, we're watching each other's back. Got it?"

"Are you saying you're here for a sleepover?"

She folded one of the pillows in half and leaned back on it. "Yep. Sure am."

"I think we're fine to stay in separate places. You'd still be close by."

"And miss out on this rare opportunity for girl time? I don't think so."

"All right, fine. If you want to stay, you can stay."

"Oh, I planned on staying whether you had a problem with it or not. And I should warn you … your brother says I snore. I don't believe it, but I figured you should know, just in case."

Fantastic.

"I had an interesting talk with Hunter before she left," I said.

"Oh, yeah. What about?"

"Seems every employee Grace has hired has a criminal history of some kind."

"How bad of a history are we talking?"

I reached for the notes Hunter gave me and handed them to her. She spent the next several minutes looking through them before handing them back to me. "Looks like we need to circle back, keep talking to the staff. Some more than others."

"We need to talk to the guests as well," I said. "I plan on bringing everyone together in the morning. After that's over, we can start one-on-one interviews."

"You talk to Clara today?"

"I never got around to it. I thought about talking to her tonight, but I'm exhausted. If I don't get a good night's sleep, I'll be worthless in the morning. I'll speak to her tomorrow, Abby too."

"What can I do?"

"I'd like you to chat with the spa sisters again," I said. "Ask them about the house they torched."

"What about Tyler, the chef?"

"He seems too soft to be a murderer, but yeah, we'd better talk to him too. I've already spoken to Calvin. No need to question him again … yet. Hunter's looking into the guests tonight. We should have more information on them in the morning."

"Sounds like we better get some sleep then. Going to be a long day tomorrow."

"I agree."

I switched off the light and leaned back.

And then there were fourteen.

Six guests, including Simone and me.

Seven staffers.

One owner.

And somewhere in that mix, one cold-blooded murderer.

24

opened my eyes and found myself sitting in the passenger seat of what appeared to be a beat-up old car. It was small and shaped like a Pinto. Maybe it was one. I couldn't be sure. I looked down and noticed I was still wearing the silk nightdress I'd worn to bed. My seatbelt wasn't fastened. I tried pulling it over my body, but it wouldn't budge. I guessed it was broken just like almost everything else seemed to be inside this car.

The floor mat beneath my feet was littered with stains—and not small stains either. Large ones. Big, black blemishes that looked like splotches of oil had leaked over parts of it, and there was a twelve-inch crack in the dashboard.

I breathed in a lungful of stale air. It smelled like cigarettes and cheap perfume. I glanced out the window. It was night but there were flashes of visibility, thanks to a hint of a crescent moon peeking through the clouds.

Where was I?

And why was I here?

It didn't take long for me to find my answer.

I *wasn't* here.

I was in a dream.

I turned to my left. The woman driving the car looked like a younger version of Quinn Abernathy. Her hands gripped the steering wheel as her eyes fixated on the road. She didn't seem to know I was there beside her. Or if she did, she hadn't acknowledged me yet.

"Quinn? Is it you?" I asked.

She didn't look my way, didn't offer any indication that she'd heard me.

"What are you doing here?" I asked. "What am *I* doing here?"

Again, she ignored me. I tapped her shoulder with a finger, hoping it would force her to acknowledge my presence, and it worked.

"Stop it," she said. "I'm trying to drive. Can't you see?"

"Where are we?"

"It doesn't matter."

"It *does* matter."

"I didn't ask you to be here. You chose to be."

"If you don't want me here, if you're not going to explain why I'm here, pull over and let me out."

Her eyes flooded with tears. "Let you out? Let yourself out. Don't you get it? None of this is real."

"I know it's not real. I have dreams like this sometimes. They're always the same. You want to show me something or tell me something or both. Which is it?"

"You don't understand."

"Then help me understand."

Tears splashed down her cheeks. We came to a stoplight, and I looked around. The surroundings looked familiar, like we were in a town I'd been in before, but I couldn't place it. One thing I knew for certain, we weren't in the present day. We were somewhere back in time. How far back, I didn't know.

We passed an old theater and then it clicked.

"Are we in Cambria?" I asked.

"You tell me."

If it was Cambria, the old theater had since been torn down, making way for a bookstore and a coffee shop.

"What year is this?" I asked.

"You're the detective. Don't you know?"

"I know we're not in the present. Something happened to you years ago. Something awful. Didn't it?"

She nodded. "An event that changed my life."

"What event?"

"Talk to Karl. He knows."

"I already talked to him," I said. "He doesn't know because you never got the chance to tell him."

A look of confusion swept across her face. She pressed a hand to her damp cheeks, wiping them dry. "I was going to tell him. It's why I went there, to talk about it, put the past in the past. You believe me, don't you?"

"I do."

"And yet, you still haven't figured it out."

"I will," I said. "I just need a little more time. Do you know who killed you?"

"Yes, but … I don't understand."

"What don't you understand?"

"Why they did it."

She turned, looking out the driver's side window, and I saw the bloody, gaping hole in her head. The dream sequence seemed to be a mashup of the present and the past.

There must be something here.

Some clue I have yet to uncover.

A clue that resided in my subconscious mind.

"Have you ever done something so terrible, so cruel, that you believed you were better off dead?" she asked. "And no matter how much you tried to turn your life around, to move on, you knew you'd never be able to forgive yourself for it."

"I have."

"Tell me about it."

"I'd rather not."

"If you don't want to speak your truth, why should I speak mine?"

She was beginning to sound a lot like Karl and Grace.

"I don't like talking about it," I said.

"Why not? It's not like I'm going to tell anyone. I'm dead."

"This isn't about me," I said. "It's about you."

"And yet, you came to the retreat too. Why?"

"I didn't know what this place was all about when I made the decision to come here."

"Yes, you did. A detective like you. You seem like the type of woman who would be on top of a thing like that, a woman who does her research."

It was the second time a comment like this had been said to me.

"This was meant to be a relaxing getaway," I said. "I do my research when it matters."

"When does it matter?"

"It matters now."

"Part of you wants to be at the retreat, but you can't admit it to yourself."

This dream was different than the ones I'd had before. A lot less informative, and a lot more combative. Perhaps my sessions with Karl had affected me more than I liked to admit. Perhaps I was off my game.

Perhaps.

I couldn't shake the feeling there was more to this dream, something I had yet to figure out. Before I could delve into it any further, Quinn slammed on the brakes, the car coming to an abrupt stop. My head smacked against the dashboard. I tried to move but couldn't. My head throbbed in pain. Time passed, blurring together, fragments of memories coming and going, flooding my mind.

Sit up.

Sit up now.

I grabbed the dashboard with both hands, forcing myself into a sitting position. I turned toward Quinn. She was beating her fists against the steering wheel, staring out at the street. She looked at me, sobbing, and said, "I'm sorry. I'm so, so sorry."

G eorgiana? Wake up."

I opened my eyes and turned to see Simone hovering over me, clutching a cup of coffee between her hands.

"What is it?" I asked. "What's going on?"

"I think you were having a bad dream. You were talking, well, more like mumbling a bunch of gibberish. I couldn't make sense of anything you were saying."

"Sorry," I said.

She raised a brow and said, "It was one of *those* dreams, wasn't it?"

Several months back, I'd admitted to Simone and Hunter that I often experienced strange dreams at times when I worked a homicide case. Simone thought it was fantastic, which wasn't a surprise. She believed in all kinds of things—spirits of the dead still lingering around after death, reincarnation, communicating with the other side. Hunter, on the other hand, saw things in black or white. If it couldn't be explained, she didn't believe it. And yet, she still indulged the possible interpretations of my dreams when I had them.

"Yes, it was one of those dreams," I said, "but also different. It was just so weird."

"Weird, how? You want to talk about it?"

"I think Quinn was in a car accident, and I think someone was in the car with her when it happened. Whoever it was, I think they died." I glanced out the window. "What time is it?"

"Almost seven."

"I need to speak to Hunter."

She nodded and sat next to me.

I made the call and put the phone on speaker.

"I was just about to call you," Hunter said. "How was it last night? Anything happen?"

"Nothing. Not that we know of, anyway."

"How are things with you?"

"A lot better now that I'm home."

I was relieved to hear it.

"I'd like you to look into something else for me today," I said. "I need to know if anything of note happened to Quinn about twenty years ago. I'm wondering if she had a car accident, and if someone was in the car with her, someone who may have died."

"What makes you think she had an accident?"

"I had an interesting dream last night. We all know there was this major event that happened in Quinn's life, something that affected her. She mentioned it to Karl, but she never got around to giving him the details. Maybe her daughter knows, but I haven't been able to speak to her yet."

"What happened in the dream?"

"I was inside a beat-up old car, somewhere in Cambria maybe. Quinn was next to me, driving. I wasn't sure where we were, but the surroundings were older. At the end of the dream, Quinn slammed on the brakes. The last thing I remember is her looking at me and saying how sorry she was, but I have no idea why she said it."

"Do you think she had an accident, or do you think you're just projecting after your conversation with Karl? Maybe your subconscious is trying to fill in the gaps you haven't been able to yet."

Maybe.

"Still, it would put my mind at ease if you could check to see if anything major happened to her all those years ago," I said. "At least then I'll know whether there's any truth to it or not."

"I understand, no problem."

"What did you find out last night during your research?"

"I looked into the remaining four guests at the retreat. I'll send over what I found in a few minutes."

"Anything I should know right now?" I asked.

"All of them are squeaky clean, run-of-the-mill types. There's Olivia, an elementary schoolteacher. She just got married a few months ago. Then there's Betsy. She's about the same age as Quinn, and she just lost her husband a few months back. I'm sure that's why she's at the retreat. Noelle is a retired postal service worker. She seems also to have a regular life, a husband, two grown daughters."

"What about the other guest—Margie?"

"I saved her for last because you're going to want to question her."

"Why? What did you find out?"

"I'm not saying she's guilty or anything, but out of everyone I've checked into, she's the only one at the retreat besides Quinn's daughter who seems to have a connection to Quinn."

"What kind of connection?"

"After our group session the first night, I was walking back to my place, and I passed Quinn. She was talking to Clara about the different businesses she's owned. She had a gift shop and before that a floral shop called The Twisted Tulip."

"What about it?"

"When I looked into Margie's employment history, I noticed she used to work at a florist called The Twisted Tulip. Can't be a coincidence, right? I mean, how many floral shops out there have a name like that?"

In my estimation, not many.

P er my request, Grace gathered everyone together, employees and guests alike. I entered the great hall and looked around. The tone was somber, all those in attendance eyeing me like they'd rather be anywhere else.

Tough crowd.

The workers had gathered in a group huddle, like bees swarming around their hive, whispering to each other. I couldn't make out much of what they were saying, but as I walked by, I heard Quinn's name.

Simone took a seat at the back of the room, and I walked to the front. I asked her to keep an eye on everyone as I spoke. I wanted her to assess everyone's body language to see if anyone was acting "off" in any way.

Grace joined me at the front and addressed all those who'd gathered. "Thank you for coming. You've all been informed about the unfortunate death of one of our guests. The police department has asked us to let you know Quinn Abernathy's death is under investigation. They're working hard to find out what happened and why. Standing next to me today is Georgiana, one of our guests, who also happens to be a private investigator. She's working with the police on this case. I've asked you here in the hopes that you'll cooperate with the investigation in every way possible. And on that note, I'll turn it over to Georgiana to say a few words."

Grace took a seat, and I began by saying, "I want to reiterate what Grace just said and thank you all for being here today. I own the Case Closed Detective Agency in Cambria. I work alongside Lilia Hunter, who couldn't be with us today, and Simone Bonet, who is seated at the back."

Heads turned, and Simone waved a quick hello.

"As you know, late Tuesday night Quinn Abernathy was found dead in her residence. We thought it best to keep the details under wraps until we had more details, but as of this moment, there's reason to believe her death was a homicide. I know this may worry some of you, but I want you to know that Simone and I are remaining here to keep an eye on things. San Luis Obispo's Chief of Police, Rex Foley, has also assigned two officers to join us, and they'll be here for the remainder of the week, if not longer."

I paused a moment to gauge their reaction, and a hand went up.

Kelly, one of the spa attendants, said, "Are you *sure* it's a homicide, or are you just guessing?"

When I worked a case like this one, it wasn't often that I gave away a lot of details. This case was different in that I believed the killer was among us now, right here in this room.

"I believe it's a homicide, yes."

"Why?"

"I'll be meeting with each of you later on, and we can talk more about that as well as address any concerns you may have."

"We're all here. Why can't we talk about it now?"

"Chief Foley will be arriving soon," I said. "He'd like me to hold off on answering too many questions until he has the chance to speak to you himself. You may be feeling frustrated and distressed, and that's understandable. While this isn't the week you all thought you'd be having, we would ask that everyone remain at the resort and cooperate with this investigation."

Kelly crossed her arms and slouched in her chair. "And if we don't want to be poked and prodded with questions? We didn't even know Quinn. Why should we care enough to get involved?"

"Quinn was a human being, just like you, with family and friends. It's up to all of us to help her get the justice she deserves."

"Are you questioning us because you want justice, or are you questioning us because y'all believe one of us is responsible for her death? You think one of *us* did it, right?"

It wasn't the way I saw the meeting going, and Kelly was wearing on what little patience I had.

"All we want to do is to ask a few questions," I said. "It's standard procedure, nothing to worry about."

"You wanna ask questions, and then what? Y'all decide who to pin the crime on?"

Kelly was coming from the place of a woman who'd been through the criminal justice system before. She'd riled everyone up, and I stood there, trying to figure out how to deescalate the situation. Karl, who'd been leaning against the wall next to Simone, walked to the front of the room and stood beside me.

He glanced at me and said, "May I?"

I nodded and stepped aside.

"Good morning, everyone. I understand you're all a little rattled by what's happening here, and that's normal," he said. "I spent some quality time with Quinn before she died. She was a woman who struggled a great deal in her life. She came here to heal, to let go of her past, and to find new beginning for herself. I believe every person in this room knows what that feels like. We've all been there at times in our lives. Just when she thought she was in the right place at the right time, making a real effort to change, her life was taken from her. And now, it's up to us to help give her the peace in death that she was never able to achieve for herself in life. We all want that for her, don't we?"

Most everyone in the room nodded.

A few did not, including Kelly, who remained resolute on sabotaging any strides we were trying to make.

"When you say *all*," Kelly said, "there are several guests missing, if I'm not mistaken."

Kelly's sister, Rebecca, wagged a finger at me, adding, "*Your* family and friends and Quinn's own daughter aren't here. Explain why it's okay for them to leave, but we should stay."

"Good question," I said. "Everyone who left did so with permission from Chief Foley. He's been keeping in touch with all of them and is following up with Quinn's daughter as we speak."

I scanned the crowd, sensing the ever-escalating tension in the room. It wouldn't be long before others joined in.

I wanted to tell them about the note that had been left on my door, about the assault on my mother, about the killer who was still out there—not just lurking but sitting here at *this* moment, in *this* room. But sharing those details would send them running.

Maybe they should flee.

Maybe I was wrong for wanting to keep them here.

Maybe by keeping them here, I was putting them all in danger.

But I didn't believe that.

I believed Quinn's death was personal and premeditated.

And I believed she was the sole target.

I also believed I'd been receiving threats because I was still here, looking around in places the killer didn't want me to be. By now, he or she knew my intentions. And if there was one thing I was sure of, it was this: the killer was within reach, and I needed to bring him, or her, to justice.

27

The meeting ended with Grace taking Kelly into the next room where they could speak in private. A few minutes later, they returned, and Kelly didn't utter another word.

Prior to the meeting, I'd spoken to Karl. We'd decided as soon as I finished talking to everyone, he'd lead them in a group session—employees and guests alike. If there was one thing I needed more than anything right now, it was to keep people close, where I could see them, observe them, eliminating them one by one until I had my killer.

Foley hadn't arrived yet, so I decided I'd get going on my own questioning. Hunter had suggested I start with Margie, but the person foremost on my mind was Clara. I'd start with her. Ever since she'd found me in Quinn's room the night of the murder, she'd been avoiding me.

According to Grace, Clara often took a thirty-minute break at this hour. I was told most days she spent her break taking walks along the path where my mother had been attacked the night before.

Sure enough, Clara was right where Grace told me she'd be.

She heard me coming and turned toward me, huffing an irritated, "What do you want?"

"You ditched out on Karl's group session."

"So."

"Why did you leave?"

"I don't like doing group stuff. You going to tell me what you want, or what?"

"I want to talk to you," I said.

"You know what seems funny to me? The one person who was in the room after Quinn died was *you*, and yet here you are, questioning us. Who's questioning you?"

If it was blunt, honest conversation she was looking for, I was ready to play ball. "Go ahead, question me. Do you think I had something to do with Quinn's death?"

"I did. I don't now. Maybe I'm wrong. Who knows?"

"What changed your mind?"

She took a seat on one of several benches dotting the tree-lined path.

I joined her.

"I overheard your mother talking about you yesterday morning, about your detective business and all the murderers you've caught over the years. She also said something about your dad and about how he was a detective too before he died. I mean, just because you have a detective agency doesn't mean you're not capable of killing someone, but I'm guessing you haven't."

"I have, but it was in self-defense."

"Figures."

"I didn't have anything to do with Quinn's death. I was just as surprised as you were when I found her."

She pulled her cardigan tighter across her chest and sighed. "It's like Kelly said. You think it's one of us, don't you?"

"It makes sense, don't you think? It's a gated retreat. No one came in or left the night Quinn died, except Grace, who went home for the evening."

"Who told you that—Calvin?"

"He did. We've also been over the security footage from that night."

"Yeah, well, it still doesn't mean one of the staffers was responsible."

"The other night when you found me in Quinn's room, you were so protective of her, a woman you'd just met," I said. "Why?"

She broke eye contact and looked away. "I don't know. I felt bad for what happened to her, I guess."

I wasn't buying it.

"I don't think I've ever met someone who's shown so much concern for a person they didn't know," I said.

She glanced at me as if trying to decide what to say. "I stopped by Quinn's place a few times to see if she needed anything, just like I did for you. She always invited me inside. She'd offer me tea or coffee. She made me feel like we were friends, even though she didn't know a thing about me."

"What did the two of you talk about?"

"Why do you want to know?"

"I'm just curious," I said.

"I'd rather not say what we discussed. They were private conversations."

"I get it, but it would be helpful if you told me. Even if you tell me what she said to you."

"Why should I?"

"Look, I'd like to think you had nothing to do with Quinn's death, but you're not making it easy."

She leaned back and ran a hand through her hair. "My break's over soon. I should get going. About Quinn and what happened to her … it wasn't me. I liked her. I mean it. She didn't treat me like a worker. She treated me like a person, like someone she wanted to get to know. It was sweet. It's amazing how much small acts of kindness can mean so much when you've lacked them all your life."

Lacked them all your life.

I wondered if it was the reason she'd resorted to stealing.

"I understand everyone who works here has been in trouble with the law at some point," I said.

"You wouldn't know a thing about what we've been through. You show up here in your fancy car with your fancy family and fancy friends. I've been on my own since I was thirteen."

"I'm sorry."

"I don't need an apology, not from someone like you."

Someone like me.

Someone she'd predetermined she couldn't connect with even if she tried.

Quinn, on the other hand, had made no attempt to hide the damage from her past. The outburst she'd had in the group session was a spectacle, even if she hadn't intended it to be one.

"I get it," I said.

"You get *what?*"

"You look at me and you pass judgment. You decide who I am, where I came from, what I'm like. Don't get me wrong. I'm guilty of it too. I suppose sometimes being critical is part of my job, but not always. There's more to me than what you see. Just because pain isn't visible on the outside doesn't mean it's not there."

She shrugged. "I guess."

"I have a good family, good friends, a good life. But there is no life without death, and death is one thing I know well. I've seen it. I've felt its darkness, the weight seeping through my insides like poison. I've had days when the loss I felt was so unbearable, I wanted to give in."

"Wow, that's, uhh … deep."

She caught my eye, and we both grinned.

"Yeah, maybe too deep," I said. "I don't talk about this stuff often."

"You seem to be in a good place now."

"I'm in a better place. The demons are still there. They'll always be, I imagine. Maybe that's why I'm in this line of work. Maybe bringing families closure helps to balance me out somehow—a ray of light to overcome the darkness."

She glanced at her watch.

"Do you need to go?" I asked.

"In about five minutes."

She'd gone from wanting to get away from me to deciding it was okay to sit a bit longer. I must have said something right.

"It's too bad I never got the chance to talk to Quinn," I said. "Seems like she was a nice person."

"I thought so. You know, the comment you made about all of us who work here being in trouble with the law ... I suppose you've researched our backgrounds. I'm not the type of person who steals. It wasn't like I was swiping clothes and jewelry and stuff."

"How did it start?"

"When I lost my job. I couldn't pay rent. I got kicked out of my place and I had nowhere to go. No money. No food. I was in a grocery store one morning right after it opened, staring at all the pastries they'd just put out, and ... I don't know. I couldn't resist. And I didn't get caught, which made it easier to do it again. And again."

"I can't imagine what that must have been like for you."

"Yeah, well, I'm just doing my best to leave it all behind. Thanks to Grace giving me a job here, for the first time in my life, I feel like I have a family."

"You're referring to your co-workers?" I asked.

"Yeah, well, most of them."

"Are there some you get along with more than others?"

"It's just like any other job. It's impossible to get along with everyone all the time."

It seemed like she was referring to a specific person.

I wondered who.

"What do you know about the crimes of your fellow employees?" I asked.

"I wouldn't call being caught selling weed a crime."

"I didn't know Tyler sold it. He seems like a gentle person. A bit on the shy side."

She tilted her head this way and that, weighing the comment. "Tyler's not shy once you get to know him."

"I heard the women who work in the spa were convicted of arson."

"Yeah, they're a feisty pair, but good people. I don't condone setting your ex's house on fire, but I know why they did it. Rebecca had been abused by her husband. When she got up the nerve to leave him, she confessed everything to Kelly, who had no idea it had been going on. In the divorce, Rebecca's ex was awarded the house, and Kelly couldn't handle seeing her sister suffer any more than she already had. She decided he needed to pay for what he'd done."

It was good information, and it resonated. If anyone put a hand on my sister, torching their house would be the least of their concerns.

"What about Abby, the other woman working in guest services? She got in a bar fight, didn't she?"

Clara rolled her eyes. "Abby's, uhh, yeah, she can be a lot sometimes. I've learned to keep my distance."

And there it was—the employee rift.

She reached into her pocket and pulled out some lip balm, and in doing so, a small crumpled-up bit of paper fell out, fluttering to the ground. I reached down to pick it up, noticing it was the same type of paper, same size and shape as the one left on my door and in my mother's pocket. I opened it, hoping to find some words written on the page, but it was blank.

I held it up to her. "What is this?"

She narrowed her eyes, looking at me like she was irritated by my question. I didn't blame her. It was only after I'd spoken that I realized my tone had been more accusatory than inquisitive. After moving the conversation into a positive, more open direction, I didn't want to revert back to square one.

I checked myself and tried again. "I've seen paper like this since I've been here, and I was just wondering where you got it."

"Why?"

I debated what to say next. If I told her the truth and she spread it around to everyone else, it might cause the type of panic I was trying to avoid. I envisioned everyone at the retreat wanting to hightail it out of here.

"If you know where the paper came from, trust me when I say it's important that you tell me," I said. "I wouldn't ask unless it wasn't."

"I found it."

"Where?"

"On the ground just a few minutes ago. It bothers me when people litter. If I see anything when I'm walking the grounds, I pick it up, pocket it, and throw it in the trash later."

"Can you show me where you found it?" I asked.

"Yeah, I guess."

The two of us walked the path back toward the living quarters. About halfway there, she stopped and said, "I think it was somewhere around here. I remember because I had to pick it out of the flower garden."

I looked where she was pointing and nodded as I realized where we were standing, not more than ten feet away from where my mother had been assaulted.

28

The paper Clara had found, *if* she had "found" it, made me curious as to how it ended up in the flowerbed, when it ended up there, and why. Perhaps it was part of a notepad, and the person responsible for attacking my mother hadn't realized a piece of it had slipped away.

I shifted my focus to Margie, one of the guests at the retreat. I was curious about the possibility she had worked for Quinn at the flower shop. I walked to her bungalow and knocked. When she answered the door, two suitcases were sitting just inside, all packed and ready to go.

"Are you going somewhere?" I asked.

"Yeah, home. I can't be here anymore. I should have left yesterday."

She rolled a hair tie off her wrist and pulled her shoulder-length, auburn mane into a loose bun. She'd been sweating, the armpits of her coral, flowy lounge dress stained with large circles, like she'd been rushing around.

"Can we talk for a minute?" I asked.

She moved a hand to her hip. "If it's quick. I'd like to get out of here."

"It would be better if you stayed."

"Better for who? You? The cops? I don't care. You can't keep me here."

"I'm not trying to keep you here."

"Yes, you are. Isn't that what your meeting was about? You and the other woman you work with, trying to convince us we're safe because *you're* here, and two more officers are on the way. I'm not sure how you think that came across, but as far as I'm concerned, you don't send officers to keep an eye on things unless there's a threat, a reason for them to be here."

I wanted to offer a rebuttal, but I couldn't.

Thinking about it from her perspective, I saw her point.

I'd thought telling everyone the chief of police was sending officers to the retreat would make them feel better about what had happened here.

I was wrong.

I wondered if everyone else felt the same way Margie did.

"Can we sit, just for a few minutes?" I asked. "And then I'll get out of your way, and you can leave."

She tapped a foot to the ground, debating. "Five minutes."

I followed her to the living room, and we sat across from each other, her on the couch, me on a chair. Knowing the clock was ticking, I dove right in. "What brought you to the retreat this week?"

"Last year, I started meditating in the morning. I tried doing it on my own at first, but it was too hard. I couldn't just sit there and clear my mind. Thoughts would seep in, and it seemed impossible to push them to the side. I almost gave up, and then I found some videos on the internet. Guided meditations. Every day, a different theme. I tried them out, and they worked. A few months later, I learned Karl, the meditational guide, worked here."

"And you decided to book in?"

"I did. I couldn't wait to meet him in person."

"We've been doing some background checks on everyone and—
"

Margie raised a hand, stopping me. "You've discovered I worked for Quinn."

"I did."

"It was a long time ago. Twenty-something years, at least. I worked there for a couple of years, and then one day she called me into the office. She said the business wasn't doing well and she couldn't afford to stay open any longer."

"Did she say why?"

"She didn't. It was strange though. One day the business was thriving, the next it wasn't."

"Why? Any idea what happened?"

"You ever talk to someone and it's like they're standing there, right in front of you, but they're somewhere else in their mind?"

"I have."

I was guilty of it myself.

"That's how I would describe her," she said. "She was a bright, smart, savvy businesswoman one day, always working hard to grow the business, and then *poof*, everything changed. She lost focus, became indifferent. I assumed it was because her marriage was falling apart at the time. Now I'm not so sure."

"What makes you think something else happened?"

"Four years after the business went kaput, she called and asked me to go to lunch. She'd booked us in at a lavish five-star restaurant. She said she'd started a new business, a gift shop, and it was doing well. She even offered me a job, but I already had one. I have to say, she looked great, like a woman with a new lease on life."

"What was discussed during lunch?"

"She apologized about the floral shop closing. I said I understood. I knew the pressure she was under, given her marriage was ending at the time."

"What did she say?"

"The oddest thing. She said the end of her marriage was hard, but it wasn't what tanked the business. There was something else.

Something she didn't want to talk about. As happy as she seemed, whatever it was, I could tell it still weighed on her mind. Since she didn't want to talk about it, I didn't press her for more information."

"Any idea what it may have been?"

She shook her head. "After our lunch, I didn't see or hear from her again until a few days ago, when I arrived here."

"Did you talk to her?"

"I tried. She didn't recognize me at first. I'll admit, I've gained some weight since the last time she saw me. My hair's a lot shorter now and a different color. Anyway, I reminded her who I was, and I assumed she'd want to catch up. She didn't. I don't think she was happy to see me."

"Why do you say that?"

"She kept trying to end the conversation, and when I saw her in the dining hall or anywhere around this place, she'd look the other way. It was obvious she was avoiding me."

Quinn had come to the retreat to work through her past, her insecurities, things she wanted to let go. I bet she intended on leaving the outside world behind, and then *bam*—she sees a blast from the past on day one.

"A lot of people come to this place to get away from it all, to work through things," I said. "Even though the last time you saw each other you had a good time catching up, maybe seeing you here had triggered her in some way."

"I'm not so sure. It may have been part of the reason, but there's more to it."

Margie knew something.

Something she hadn't said.

"Is there anything about Quinn that I should know before you go?" I asked. "Anything that could help me with the investigation?"

"There is *one* thing … her real name? It isn't Quinn."

29

Quinn isn't her real name?" I asked.

"Nope. I don't think so, anyway. When I knew her, she went by Brynn."

Interesting.

Margie stood and walked to the kitchen. "All this talking has me parched. You thirsty?"

"I'm fine, thanks."

Margie gulped down a glass of water, refilled it, and returned to the sofa. She took a few sips from the glass, set it down on a coaster, and continued. "When I worked at the floral shop, she went by Brynn Fielding, and I never heard anyone call her by any other name. The surname changed because she remarried. That part makes sense. But I don't get why she changed her first name too."

"When did you realize she'd changed it? After you arrived here?"

"It was before, during the fancy lunch we had. When the check came, she signed it Quinn instead of Brynn. She did it fast. I'm guessing she hoped I wouldn't notice, but I did."

"Did you ask her about it?"

She shook her head. "I assumed I'd read it wrong. That happens with signatures sometimes. I suppose I didn't think about it much after that until I got here and overheard her being called Quinn."

It may have been the reason Quinn was uncomfortable seeing Margie.

But was it the only reason?

"When I saw her at the beginning of the week, I asked her why she was going by a different name," Margie said.

"What was her answer?"

"She brushed it off by saying Quinn was a nickname she'd been called as a kid. Doesn't that seem odd to you though? Doesn't seem like a nickname a person would have when your first name is Brynn."

"You're right. That is odd. Where was the floral shop located?"

"San Francisco."

"And did Quinn live in the city too?"

"All of her adult life, from what she told me."

"Did she have any children at the time?"

Margie shook her head.

"What about her parents?" I asked. "Did she ever mention them?"

"Here and there. Back then, they lived in Cambria. I believe that's where she grew up."

"That's where I live now. Were her parents still alive when you worked together?"

"When we met up for lunch, she said her dad had passed. I don't know if her mother's still alive."

"Quinn has a daughter named Faith. She was also at the retreat this week."

Margie pressed a hand to her chest. "I had no idea Faith was her daughter. Nice girl. I chatted with her for a few minutes earlier in the week."

"No one here knew Faith was Quinn's daughter," I said. "Not until after she died."

"All of this … it seems mighty strange to me."

"Me too," I said. "Back when you worked together, did Quinn have any enemies?"

"I don't believe so."

"What did you do after the floral shop closed?"

"I spent some time off the grid. And by off the grid, I mean I went back to help my family on their farm for a while. Didn't have any communication with the outside world for a long time."

"Why?"

"Why not? Sometimes it's good to unplug. Speaking of unplugging…"

Margie's phone buzzed and she stood. "Well, I better scoot. I told my husband I'd call him when I left, and that was supposed to be twenty minutes ago."

I thanked Margie for her time and asked if she'd leave me her contact information, which she did. I walked out the door thinking about how forthcoming she'd been, how pleasant. Maybe a little *too* pleasant.

30

left Margie's place and gave Hunter a call. She did a quick search and confirmed what I'd suspected. After closing the floral shop, Quinn had moved away from San Francisco. Six months later, she married, changing both her given name and her surname. A year later, Faith was born. Quinn's mother died a year after her father.

After we ended the call, I stopped by Grace's office to ask a few more questions. I found her with her feet kicked up on top of her desk, head back. A thick, damp cloth was draped over her face. In the corner of the room, a diffuser was pumping a fine mist into the air. It smelled like lemon and lavender.

"Are you all right?" I asked.

She pulled the cloth to the side and peeked up at me. "No, I'm not. They're gone."

"What do you mean they're gone. *Who's* gone?"

She removed the cloth, tossed it into a wastebasket, and sat up. "The guests. All of them left after the meeting this morning. Aside from you and Simone, my employees are all that remain. And I suppose they're still here because they have nowhere else to go. Even so, part of me is worried they'll leave too."

I took a seat across from her. "Your employees are the reason I'm here. I have a few questions."

"Go on."

"I hear everyone in your employ has a criminal history of some kind."

She folded her hands over her lap and nodded. "You're right. All of them have gotten into a bit of trouble at one time or another. Nothing too major."

"You don't worry one of them could slip, causing a situation in front of your guests?"

"It isn't a big concern of mine, no."

"Why not?"

"Do you believe in second chances?"

Second chances were a gray area.

"It depends on the person," I said. "Some people deserve a second chance. Some don't."

"I believe most people deserve a second chance. We're all human. We all make mistakes."

"What made you decide to hire people who have been in trouble with the law?"

"I know how hard it can be for some of them to get jobs after serving time. Nowadays almost every job application asks about a criminal record, even fast-food restaurants, if you can believe it. I'm sure there are those who would dismiss such a person, no matter how big or small the crime. I'd like to think we help them move on from the person they were to the person they can become."

It seemed helping wounded birds was her life's work.

Part of me admired her for it.

The other part thought she was a bit too "glass half full" all the time. I wondered if she'd considered the dangers involved with bringing on some of the more aggressive staff like Rebecca, Kelly, and Abby. Not everyone can be saved.

"I'm not sure what to do now," Grace said. "New guests are due to arrive on Monday, and Chief Foley has just asked me to cancel their reservations while he continues questioning everyone."

"I'm doing everything I can to solve this case so you can keep your doors open. How long can you last without accepting more guests?"

"The retreat has done well over the last year. We're booked to full capacity every week now. I've been able to set aside a bit of money in case of an emergency. It should be enough to keep this place up and running for a few weeks, maybe a little more. If I can't accept new guests by then … well, I'd rather not think about it."

"Foley won't ask you to stay closed any longer than is necessary. He just wants to make sure it's safe."

"She's right." I turned to see Foley standing in the doorway. He poked his head in, looked at me, and said, "Georgiana, we need to talk."

31

oley and I walked over to my bungalow, engaging in small talk until we stepped inside and found Simone leaning back on the sofa, staring at something on her cell phone. She smiled at me and said, "How are you doing, after the … you know, what happened this morning?"

Foley took a seat on a barstool. "What happened this morning?"

"I guess I scared all the guests away with my pep talk," I said.

He shook his head. "Why am I not surprised?"

"I don't get it," I said. "I thought talking to them would put them at ease. It did the opposite."

"It was a tough crowd," Simone said.

"Just a thought," Foley said. "Next time you decide to have a chat with a group of people during a murder investigation, consider letting me do the talking."

He'd said it in the nicest possible way, but I knew what he was suggesting.

His way of dealing with people was a lot different than mine.

"With all the guests gone, I think it's best if I pull my officers,"

Foley said. "Their time will be better spent working on this case from the department. You all right with that?"

I nodded.

Simone did the same.

"Did you talk to Faith this morning?" I asked.

"I did."

"How's she doing? How's the baby?"

"Baby's fine, but I get the impression Faith's not."

"I'm sure she's still reeling over what happened to her mother."

"Her phone's been ringing nonstop since family and friends learned about Quinn's death."

"What else did she say?" Simone asked.

"It seems Quinn was a private person, even when it came to her own daughter. Faith said she doesn't know much about her mother's life prior to her birth."

"What did she say about her relationship with her mother?" I asked.

"They'd been through their share of ups and downs over the years, but when Faith told Quinn she was trying to get pregnant, Quinn promised she'd be there for them both."

And then she died, without even having the chance to redeem herself.

What a shame.

"I wonder why Quinn felt she needed to make a promise like that to her," Simone said.

"Ask me, Quinn was worried Faith wouldn't want her around the baby all that much," Foley said.

"Why not?" I asked.

"Quinn battled with depression from time to time. For years, Faith asked her to get help, but she resisted."

"Coming to the retreat was a big step for her then," I said.

"A giant scissor-step in the right direction that ended up being the wrong one," Simone said.

Moving the conversation in a different direction, I said, "Turns out one of the guests who was here this week knew Quinn."

"Seems like a big coincidence," Foley said. "Did she know Quinn was going to be here?"

"She didn't."

"How did she know her?"

"She worked at Quinn's flower shop … and get this, her real name isn't Quinn. It's Brynn."

"Huh. Wonder why she changed her name."

"In my opinion, a person doesn't change their name on a whim. They almost always have a compelling reason. Now that we know her given name, I'm hoping we'll learn a lot more about who she was back then."

"If you learn anything useful, let me know. Hey, did you know Faith's stepdad committed suicide? Guess he hung himself the day after Quinn served him with divorce papers."

"I'd heard, yes," I said. "I bet that caused a rift with his family members."

"I'm sure it did. Something we'll follow up on."

"What about the message written in lipstick in Quinn's bathroom? Did Faith know about it?"

"Claims she didn't."

"The day she died, Quinn talked to Karl about her relationship with her daughter. She expressed some regrets, and he suggested she talk to Faith. I don't know if she did."

"Quinn spoke to her. Guess she couldn't get much out as far as words go. She became real emotional and kept apologizing for not being a better mother. She didn't know how to make it up to her, but she wanted to try."

"What was Faith's reaction?" Simone asked.

"Faith strikes me as a no-nonsense kind of gal. I'm sure she offered her mother support, but she said she's not one to dwell on the past. All she wanted was to move forward."

"Did Faith know her mother had thought about leaving the retreat and called a friend to come get her?" I asked.

"She didn't. The woman's name is Jane Holland. Guess she's been good friends with Quinn since they were kids."

"Which means we should have a conversation with her."

"I agree. I stopped by her place after I left Faith's house. She wasn't home. I'll try again later."

I made a mental note to speak with the woman myself. If she'd known Quinn most of her life, there was a good chance she'd have answers to my questions.

32

I approached Karl's bungalow and saw Abby walk out. Her shirt wasn't buttoned all the way up, exposing part of her bra, and her hair was disheveled. She met my gaze and grabbed at her shirt, pulling it closed. I started to say something, but she turned, speedwalking in the opposite direction.

Karl was sitting on the floor with his legs crossed. His face was flushed and red, which didn't surprise me. Nothing like a little sex to get one's heart rate up.

"Georgiana, hi," he said. "Can you give me just a moment to—"

No.

I couldn't.

"Is having sex with one of your coworkers part of your therapy services?" I asked.

"It's not what you think."

"Isn't it? Because it looks to me like you and Abby just had sex. Are you saying you didn't?"

"I'm saying Abby's not just my coworker. We're together. We have been for some time now."

"Why the secrecy?" I asked.

"When it comes to the guests, we find it best to keep our private lives private."

And yet guests were encouraged *not* to keep their private lives private.

"Having sex in broad daylight inside a place where anyone can walk in doesn't seem that private to me," I said.

"The door was locked, and you and Simone are the only guests left from what I understand."

He had a point.

Besides, who was I to give him grief over a little horizontal tango?

He pushed himself to a standing position and walked out of the room. A couple of minutes later, he returned wearing a different shirt, and he'd slicked his shoulder-length hair back into a ponytail. He made two cups of tea and then sat down, motioning for me to do the same. "Please, join me. What can I do for you?"

"I have a few more questions about Quinn."

"We can discuss Quinn," he said, "but while you're here, why not take a moment to talk about you."

What was it with these people?

We were in the middle of a murder investigation.

How *I* was feeling could wait.

"What about me?" I asked.

He leaned in. "How are you holding up? You've spent these past days focusing on the case. Have you taken any time for yourself?"

"I'll take time for myself when the case is solved."

He reached out, grabbing my hands.

Not this again.

"Let's take a moment to discuss how you're doing," he said. "Not long. Just a moment. You'll feel better. I promise."

"I feel fine."

"Why don't you close your eyes for me?"

"No, thanks," I said.

For all I knew, Karl was the killer.

If I closed my eyes, there was no telling what he'd do.

I pulled back, releasing my hands from his. "I'm fine, Karl. Am I disappointed that I scared all the guests away this morning? Sure. I know the way I approach people isn't always right. It's hard for me to accept when it isn't."

"Why?"

"I don't like to fail, at anything."

"Does the fact they decided to leave mean you're a failure?"

"I failed to keep them here, which was the opposite of my intention."

He crossed his arms and nodded. "What is success without failure? Do you think it's better to try and fail, or never to try at all?"

"I think it's better to succeed."

He smacked a hand to his knee, laughing. "If you had a reset button, a way to go back to this morning and do it all again, knowing what you know now, what would you change?"

A few things.

"Instead of talking the entire time, telling them what I thought they wanted to hear, I should have asked how they were feeling," I said. "I should have given them a chance to voice their concerns first. Rebecca tried, and all I could think about was how fast I could shut her down before she convinced the others to do the same thing." A broad smile crossed Karl's face. "You've given it some thought."

"It's been on my mind all day."

"To me, true failure comes when one doesn't care about learning from their experiences. *You* care, and that makes all the difference. Life isn't about being perfect. It's about growth, slow and continuous. The rabbit in its haste to win the race misses what the turtle takes the time to see."

"I ... thank you, Karl."

"Thank *you*, Georgiana, for opening up to me again."

Moving on.

"You said Quinn never got the chance to open up to you about some of the pain from her past, but is there anything she may have said that you haven't already told me?" I asked.

He paused to give my question some thought. "I believe I've said everything that comes to mind. Why do you ask?"

"One of the other guests knew Quinn many years ago. When I spoke with her, she told me Quinn used to go by a different name. I'm trying to figure out if there was an event in Quinn's life that prompted the name change."

"Did this other guest give you the name?"

"Brynn," I said.

"B. Well, that's interesting."

"Why?"

"When Quinn arrived for her second session, she was carrying what I believe was a journal."

"What did it look like?"

"It was old. Its cloth cover was ripped at the edges, like it had been opened and closed many times over the years. Toward the end of the session that day, she opened it. From where I was sitting, I could have read what was written on the page, but I didn't. It was for her to decide when to share passages with me, or if she shared them at all. Since she had the book with her, I thought she might mention it, but she just snapped it shut, shaking her head and saying, 'Another day, another day.'"

"Why didn't you share this with me before?"

"I guess I figured the police would have found the journal in her bungalow."

"I don't believe they did," I said. "They never found her cell phone either."

"I mention it now because you said her name used to be Brynn. On the cover of the journal was the letter B, big, in cursive writing. I remember wondering what the B stood for … and now, it looks like we know."

33

, ahh … wanted to apologize," I said.

I was sitting on a sofa in the spa's waiting room, chatting with Kelly and Rebecca.

Kelly moved a hand to her hip. "For what?"

"This morning. I should have validated your concerns, and I didn't."

"Yeah, well, you're right. You didn't."

"I know, that's why I'm here."

"It's not the only reason you're here though, is it?"

"You're right. I was hoping to speak to you and your sister."

Kelly threw her hands up in the air. "Well, everyone's gone, so it's not like we don't have the time. Right, Rebecca?"

Rebecca nodded.

"What are your questions?" Kelly asked.

"I heard you both served time for arson."

"Should have just been me serving time, but the judge wouldn't listen to a word I said," Kelly said. "Rebecca was with me the night her ex's house went up in flames, but she wasn't there for the reason everyone assumed. She wasn't trying to help me. She was trying to stop me."

"It's true," Rebecca said.

"I get it," I said to Kelly. "You wanted payback for how he treated your sister. But to burn down his entire house? Seems extreme."

"You ever been cheated on in your own bed before?" Kelly asked.

"I haven't."

"When I found out what he'd done, all I could think about was that bed. My sister's bed, her pillows, *her* sheets—sheets we'd picked out together right before her wedding. So, yeah, I lit that baby on fire. Didn't even stop to think that I might burn down the rest of the house in the process."

"Was it the first time you've had problems controlling your anger?"

"I see what you're getting at. See right through you, matter of fact. You want to know if I am capable of murder."

"Are you?" I asked.

"No, I'm not. Why would I murder a woman I don't even know after all I've been through? Why would any of us who work here do it? My guess? It's one of the guests. That's who y'all should be looking at."

"Any guest in particular?"

"No one comes to mind. I'm just saying … we're not the right tree to be barking up."

"Did Quinn spend much time at the spa?"

Rebecca laughed. "Every free second she had. Those first couple of days, she was in here more than anyone else."

"Did she say anything out of the ordinary when she visited, or maybe do anything that seemed odd?"

Rebecca and Kelly exchanged glances, leading me to believe she had.

"Sometimes she'd fall asleep when she was in here being worked on," Kelly said. "I'd never seen a woman so tired in all my life. One time she was passed clean out. She started talking, you know, in her sleep."

"What did she say?"

"She was having a nightmare, saying something about how she didn't mean to do it, kept saying she was sorry."

"Did she say why she was sorry?"

"Nope. Rebecca came in to ask me a question, and it startled Quinn. Woman shot straight up, looking around like she didn't know where she was for a second. It was weird."

"Did you ask her about it?"

"I asked her if she was all right. She wanted to know why I asked, so I told her what I'd heard."

"And what did she say?"

"The oddest thing. She said she believed nightmares came to people who needed to atone for their sins."

34

Abby stood in the doorway of her studio apartment with a towel wrapped around her petite frame. She stared up at me, ran a hand through her short mohawk, and sighed.

"Been wondering when you'd show up," she said.

"Do you have a few minutes to talk?"

"I have nothing to say except this—I didn't kill Quinn."

"Noted. Can I come in?"

She swung the door all the way open and turned, walking away without saying another word. I stepped inside, pausing to look at her collection of black cat figurines.

"The cat I've seen wandering around here … is it yours?" I asked.

She shrugged. "I guess. I found her slinking around the property right after I started here. Grace said she didn't belong to anyone and that I could keep her if I wanted. Wouldn't say she's much of a house cat, but I set food and water out for her."

I pointed at the figurines. "Seems like you've gotten attached, to … what do you call her?"

"Wednesday. And yeah, maybe I am, but I've been collecting cat stuff for a while. She's my third. You have pets?"

"I do. A Samoyed named Luka."

"What kind of dog is a Samoyed?"

I whipped out my phone and showed her.

"Beautiful," she said.

"Thanks, I think so too."

Abby opened a dresser drawer, grabbed a tank top and some cutoff jean shorts, and released the towel. It slid down her body, puddling at her feet. Then she proceeded to get dressed right in front of me. The girl had grit.

After she dressed, she walked past me, rolled the kitchen window open all the way, and took a seat at the table.

"You can sit if you want," she said. "Mind if I smoke?"

I minded, but if I wanted her to talk, I needed to oblige.

"I wasn't aware you could do that kind of thing here," I said, flicking my fingers in the direction of the pack of smokes.

Abby grabbed a cigarette and a lighter out of a tin box on the table and lit up. "What you're supposed to do and what you can get away with are two different things, right?"

As the words were spoken, she bit down on her lip, aware of the implication she'd just placed on herself. "I'm talking about sneaking a cigarette here and there is all. You know that, right?"

"I do. Does Karl know you smoke?"

"I think so. He's never said anything to me about it. It's not like I do it all the time. I just smoke here and there when I'm stressed."

"Are you stressed?" I asked.

"Aren't you?"

I crossed one leg over the other. "No."

"Why?"

"Why should I be?" I asked.

"I dunno. Maybe it's different for you because you're around death more than the average person. Makes me uncomfortable, knowing someone died here, and no one knows why. Been sleeping with a knife under my mattress just in case."

"How long have you been dating Karl?"

She snorted a laugh. "We're not dating. We just hang out sometimes, enjoy one another's company, if you know what I mean."

"He told me you're together and have been for a while."

"Huh. Guessing he said that because you saw me leaving his place half dressed, and he was trying to be respectful of what you might think about that. I mean, I like him and all, but it's just a bit of fun. I doubt he's taking what we're doing any more serious than I am."

"He's a lot older than you."

She shot me a wink. "Yeah, and a lot more experienced."

I was starting to feel uncomfortable, a feeling I didn't have often.

"The bar fight you got into, the one that sent you to jail … was it your first?" I asked.

"My third."

She smiled like she considered it an achievement.

"Would you say you tend to lose your temper a lot?" I asked.

"Used to, I guess."

"What changed?"

"I'm sober, for starters. Over a year now. Figure another six months oughta be enough to convince my mother to let me see my …"

She glanced out the window, leaving me wondering what she was about to say.

"Convince your mother to let you see your what?" I asked.

"Not a *what*. A *who*. My daughter. She's six. My mother has full custody."

"Are you trying to regain custody?"

"That's the plan."

"How does your mother feel about that?"

"She still has a hard time trusting I won't relapse, but she's been out here a few times, seen the good we do for people, and we've been working through our issues."

Kind of like Quinn had been working through hers.

Until she wasn't.

"Are you making any progress?" I asked.

She took a few more drags off her cigarette and then snuffed the butt out on a plate. "Some."

"Did you have any interaction with Quinn?"

"A little. The night Quinn died, I saw her out walking. Looked like she'd come from the front of the property. She was bawling her eyes out. I asked her if everything was okay and if there was anything I could do for her. She thanked me, but said no. Before she walked away, she asked if I'd seen Faith, and I hadn't. Seemed odd that she asked about another guest until we learned Faith was her daughter. Makes sense now."

"How so?" I asked.

"I shouldn't say. Client privilege and all. I don't want to get in trouble."

"Quinn is dead, and your boss hired me to find out why. Whatever client privilege you think you need to protect, you don't."

She tapped a fingernail against the tabletop, thinking.

I waited.

"All right. Fine. I was walking by Faith's room the night Quinn died. Her window was open, and she was talking to someone on the phone—at least I think so, because I didn't hear anyone else talking but her. She was upset."

"About what?"

"I don't know. I heard her say she should have never agreed to come to the retreat."

"Why not?"

"Because her mother wasn't handling it well, and she was tired of talking to her about it. At first, I thought her mother must have been calling her all the time, bugging Faith when she was trying to get some time to herself."

"Any idea who she was talking to on the phone?" I asked.

She shook her head. "I felt weird standing there, hearing what I did. I'm no eavesdropper. As soon as I realized the conversation was personal in nature, I kept on walking."

"And you didn't hear her say anything else?"

Abby glanced back out the window and then leaned closer to me, lowering her voice as she said, "As I was walking away, I overheard her say she wanted to go home. She regretted coming here and thought it was a huge mistake."

35

B ut she didn't go home." Simone said. "She showed up on her mother's doorstep the next morning, ready to go for a walk."

It was three in the afternoon, and Simone and I were alone in the dining hall, catching up after a private lunch for two. Since we were the only guests left at the retreat, the usual dining times had been scrapped, and we were able to eat when it suited us.

"You're right, she didn't," I said. "It means she either calmed down after the phone call and decided to stay, or …"

"Or she just moved up on our suspect list."

"Right."

I wanted to believe she had nothing to do with Quinn's death. That when I saw her that morning, she hadn't staged the whole thing to make herself look innocent.

"She couldn't have staged the spotting, right?" I asked. "The blood, it was real. I'm sure of it."

"I'm thinking it was real. But hey, she could have started spotting because of how stressed she became after learning who you were and everything you knew about the murder. I bet she had a key to her mother's place."

"Maybe. We don't know where she's been or what she's been doing since she left here. We only know what we've been told."

"So, now what?"

"Now I talk to her myself, look her in the eye, see if I can get a feel for whether she's lying or telling the truth," I said.

Simone made a face. It wasn't a good one either.

"We need to think about the baby," she said. "Faith is still in her first trimester. She's going through a lot of hormonal changes. Any additional stress won't help."

"You're right. The last thing I want to do is upset her again."

Simone reached over, squeezed my hand. "You know I love you, right?"

I knew.

I also knew what she was getting at.

"You don't think I should talk to her, do you?" I asked.

"If she wasn't in the early stages of pregnancy, I'd say have at it. Given she is, maybe it would be best if I talk to her. What do you think?"

Delegating wasn't my strong suit, and it never would be, but Simone was right. If something happened to Faith because of a conversation I had with her, and she lost the baby, I couldn't forgive myself.

"I think you're right," I said. "Go talk to her."

Simone nodded, then added, "Oh, I almost forgot to tell you, I spoke to Hunter while you were gone. She tried to call you, but you didn't pick up. She has news."

I took my phone out of my pocket. Simone was right. I had a missed call from her about an hour before.

"What news?" I asked.

"I'm not sure. She said she wants to tell you herself. She was all hyped up on the phone. Whatever it is, I'm guessing it's juicy."

"Let's head back to my place and call her."

We made a beeline for the front door, stopping when we heard the distinct, blood-curdling sound of someone screaming.

36

We followed the scream we'd heard to one of the staff rooms, where we found the door ajar, and Chef Tyler sobbing and rocking Clara in his arms. Blood was on his shirt, his hands, his shoes—everywhere.

I scanned the room and saw a gun resting on the floor, a few feet from where Tyler stood. Simone and I exchanged glances. I thought about reaching for my own gun, but my gut instinct told me to wait.

"Tyler, I'm going to need you to back away from Clara," I said. "Right now."

"You don't understand," he said. "I didn't do anything."

I approached and knelt, assessing Clara's wound. Unlike Quinn's, Clara had been shot in the chest. She wasn't moving, wasn't breathing. I checked for a pulse. There wasn't one.

"You need to listen to Georgiana," Simone said, "and back away from Clara. Okay?"

He shook his head over and over again. "She was my friend. I would never hurt her."

"I'm not saying you would. But this is a crime scene now."

He removed a hand from the back of her head, lowering her to the floor with the utmost tenderness and care. As he stood, he stared at his bloodied hands, and burst into tears. He took one step back, then another and another until he reached the wall and slid down it, burying his head in his hands.

"I know you're shaken up, and it may be a struggle to talk about it right now," I said. "But I need you to tell me what happened and how you came to be here, in Clara's room."

He started to speak a few times and then stopped, clearing his throat each time as if it would help the words come when they didn't.

"We were … we were, ah … supposed to meet up and go for a hike together after I finished serving lunch. She didn't show up at our meeting spot, so I came looking for her, and that's when … that's when … I walked into her place and I … I …"

"Found her?" I asked.

"Yeah."

"How long ago did you get here?" I asked.

"Umm, right before you did."

"Did you see anyone on your way over here? Anyone coming or going?"

"No."

"Was Clara alive when you walked in?"

"No."

"Was the door open?" I asked.

"No."

"And you just walked into her place when she didn't come to the door?"

"It was unlocked, so … yeah."

I glanced at the time. It was almost four in the afternoon. "We saw you in the dining hall about forty-five minutes ago. You cleared our plates. When were you supposed to meet Clara?"

"About ten minutes ago."

"When was the last time you saw her?" I asked.

"This morning, around ten, when she came to get breakfast."

"How did she seem?"

"Fine, I guess. She wasn't there long. Took her breakfast to go and we made plans to meet up later, like I told you." He paused, then added, "She did say something on her way out, something I hadn't thought of until now. She said she needed to tell me something, needed my advice. I assumed that's why she asked me to go for a walk."

"Did she give you any other details?"

He shook his head.

He seemed to be telling the truth, but people weren't always as they seemed. For all I knew, he could have been trying to cover up the scene when we walked in. If so, I figured he would've had the smarts to close the door to her place, and he hadn't.

A second possibility sprung to mind.

I yanked my phone out of my pocket and dialed Faith's number. The call went to voicemail. I tried again. This time the call was answered, but it was a husky male voice on the other end.

"Who's this?" I asked.

"Who's this?"

"Georgiana Germaine," I said. "Is this Faith's fiancé?"

"Yep."

"I need to speak with Faith. It's important."

"She's not here."

A convenient answer.

But was it the truth?

"If she's not there, why are you answering her phone?" I asked.

"Why does it matter?"

"It matters because it's not your phone."

"Not my problem if she left it here. What's it to you, anyway?"

"Cut the shit, dude, and tell me where she is right now."

"Did you ever think she left her phone behind because every

cop in this town can't seem to leave her alone ever since her mother died?"

"Look, I don't have time to volley back and forth with you," I said. "You can either tell me where she is, or my next call is to the cops. I should also mention I'll be asking them to head on over to your place to have a little chat."

"About what … the dangers of leaving a phone behind?"

He laughed.

I didn't.

"Do you two live together?" I asked.

"Not yet."

"Why are you in her house if you don't live together?"

"I have a key to her place, and she has a key to mine. I'm hanging up."

"Wait … a guest services worker at the retreat is dead."

Silence, for once, on the other end of the line.

"Hello?" I asked. "You still there?"

"I'm here. What happened?"

"She was shot, just like Quinn."

"Yeah, well, Faith wouldn't know anything about it. She's at the grocery store."

"Which one?"

"I'm not sure."

"*Which* one?"

A long sigh, and then, "Peterson's Market, I think."

"How long ago did she leave?" I asked.

"I dunno. I was at work. She left me a note."

"On what kind of paper?"

"Why the hell does it matter?"

"Trust me, it does."

"Pink paper with lines on it. Okay?"

"When you see her, tell her to call me. She has my number." I ended the call and turned toward Simone, who had just dialed 911 to report the incident. "Will you find Grace and let her know I'd like to gather everyone together? I want to know what everyone has been doing over the last hour."

"You got it."

Simone headed for the front door, jolting to a stop right before she reached it. She leaned over, glancing at a piece of paper on the counter, a piece of paper that looked just like the one left on my door days earlier.

"You need to take a look at this, Gigi," she said.

I joined her, my eyes coming to rest on what appeared to be a suicide note, written in cursive handwriting.

I'm sorry for everything. For lying, for the deception, and for hurting those I care about. The truth is, I met Quinn a couple of years ago. I applied to work at her gift shop. I told her I'd served time for theft, and she wouldn't hire me because "once a thief, always a thief." She said she couldn't trust me.

After I was hired to work at the retreat, I started having sessions with Karl. As I talked about Quinn and the way she'd treated me, I was so angry. I found her address and sent her information on this place so I could confront her.

She didn't even recognize me when she got here. Every conversation was all about her. Her problems. Her life. She'd been wronged, not the other way around. I listened to her moan and complain, dumping all her issues on me like I wanted to hear her entire life story, and I just … I snapped.

I wanted to make her understand, make her say she was sorry. I knew Calvin kept a spare gun in a drawer in his place, and I borrowed it, and I shot her. I thought I could find a way out of this, but now I know I can't. I'm sorry. It's a genuine regret, a careless error on my part.

I won't be locked up again. I barely survived it the last time.

The way I see it, there's only one way out, and I've decided to take it.

Forgive me, Clara

It made sense and it didn't at the same time.

Killing someone over not being given a job?

There had to be more to it.

Right?

"Tyler," I said, "have you ever seen Clara's handwriting?"

He nodded. "She gave me a card a few weeks ago for my birthday. Why?"

"Can you come over here?"

He was reluctant, but he did as I asked.

"I know this won't be easy, and I'm sorry," I said. "Can you take a look at this note? I'm wondering if you recognize the handwriting."

"Oh-kay."

He started reading and then stopped, turning away as the tears came. "I can't read any more of this … it's too hard. But yeah, it looks like her handwriting."

"Do you still have the card?"

He nodded. "It's on my desk at my place."

"I need to look at it."

"Yeah, okay."

"I'll walk over with him," Simone said.

I nodded. "And I'll call Foley."

37

oley and Silas and his crew headed my way, along with a couple of officers. In the meantime, I did some poking around inside Clara's place, careful not to disturb any relevant evidence. Clara was wearing a pair of jogging shorts and a T-shirt when she died. Half of her breakfast was uneaten and was sitting on the counter in the kitchenette. A load of laundry had been washed but not dried. And her staff uniform was folded at the end of the bed like she intended to change back into it later.

If what Tyler said was true, it seemed odd to me that at some point between breakfast, the time we chatted, and now, she'd made the hasty decision to kill herself. And why hadn't Calvin mentioned he had a gun and that it was missing? I had a hard time believing he hadn't noticed after learning how Quinn died.

None of it was sitting right with me.

Not the suicide note.

Not her reasons for killing Quinn.

None. Of. It.

For starters, it was a coincidence that one of Quinn's former coworkers just happened to be at the retreat the same week she was, and now I was supposed to believe one of the workers at the retreat had a past history with Quinn too?

Then again, maybe Clara's story *was* true, and she planned to confess everything to Tyler, the one person she thought she could trust.

I stood there, staring down at Clara, talking to her even though she couldn't talk back. "I wish you were still here. I wish you could talk to me, tell me what happened, what you planned on telling Tyler. You were just getting your life back together. I can't believe you'd throw it away now, not over something as petty as a woman not hiring you after you got out of jail."

I heard footsteps behind me, and I turned.

"You always speak to the dead?" Foley asked.

"Sometimes."

Silas walked in behind him and headed right for me, giving me a quick squeeze. "Sure got a lot on your plate this week. You doing all right?"

"I'll be better when you can tell me whether she shot herself or not, because right now, I'm not buying it." I shifted my focus to Foley. "Did one of your officers stop by Faith's house?"

"Sure did. She was unloading groceries. She had the receipt from the store, which proved she was there during the time I'd imagine Clara was killed." He paused, then said, "Where's the suicide note?"

I pointed it out, and he headed in that direction.

Silas approached Clara and bent down, assessing her, and then the area surrounding her body. He stared at the gun for a while, and then nodded.

"What are you thinking?" I asked.

"I'm thinking the gun is the same one used to kill Quinn. Shoots the same type of bullets as the one Higgins found."

"Do you have any more information on the bullet?"

"We've examined its lands and grooves."

"And ridges and valleys," I said more to myself than anyone else.

I knew these markings were made when the bullet passed through the barrel of the gun. When fired, the markings were imparted on the gun, and the bullet itself.

"What you're saying is, you can compare distinct markings on the bullet with the gun to know whether that bullet was fired by this gun?"

"More or less, yeah."

"What about the way she's positioned? Can you tell whether she herself pulled the trigger?"

He turned toward Clara. "A lot of factors to consider. The first thing I look for is the same thing you look for—overt indications that a struggle took place—defensive wounds, other signs of a struggle, things like that. I haven't noticed anything out of the ordinary so far, but that's just preliminary. What about you? See anything odd?"

"She washed a load of laundry but didn't dry it. If she planned on offing herself, why bother washing anything?"

"Good point. What was in the wash?"

"Clothes, a couple of towels, a few other things."

"You see her around today?"

"Yeah, this morning," I said. "She'd been giving me the cold shoulder all week, but today I thought we turned a corner. She was in a decent mood at the end of our conversation. I thought she was, at least."

Foley asked one of the officers to bag the suicide note, and then he joined us.

"I have a question," I said. "When you processed Quinn's place, did you ever find a journal? It was old and had the letter B on the front."

"Nope," Foley said. "Why?"

"Karl said Quinn was carrying it with her on the day she died," I said. "And there's something I just realized. If Calvin was convicted for assault, whether he's guilty or not, he'd be banned from possessing a firearm for life, wouldn't he?"

"Should be."

"I'll bet he knows his gun is missing. I'm also guessing it's not registered. Not to him."

Foley sighed, shaking his head. "Guess we better speak to him, see what he has to say for himself."

While the scene was being processed, Foley and I met with Calvin and Grace in her office. After telling Calvin about Clara, he hung his head and remained quiet. I handled it all right for the first minute, but as the silence lingered like trapped air in a musty room, I started to unravel.

I flipped through a few photos on my phone and turned it around, facing him.

"Does this gun belong to you?" I asked.

He glanced at it, then at me, and bit down on his lip.

It did belong to him, which we all suspected.

"You had so many opportunities to tell me you had a firearm," I said. "But you didn't."

He shrugged. "You know why I didn't."

"Because you're not supposed to own a firearm. So, whose is it?"

"It's mine."

"Is it registered?" I asked.

"No."

I didn't bother asking where it came from.

There were plenty of places to acquire a piece like his on the street.

"Do you know the kind of trouble you're in?" Foley asked.

"Sure do."

"Let's back up," I said. "I'm assuming you knew the gun was missing. When did you realize it was gone?"

"Monday."

"*Before* any guests arrived on the property?"

"I'm not sure if it was before anyone arrived or after."

"Did you tell anyone?"

"Nope. Thought if I did, I might lose my job."

"You should have trusted me," Grace said. "We could have worked it out … together. Now … well, I don't know what we do now."

"Where did you keep the gun?" I asked.

"In my nightstand drawer."

"After you noticed the gun was missing, did you try to find it?" I asked.

"When I realized it wasn't there, I didn't see the point in looking around my own place. I didn't misplace it."

He may not have seen the point in looking around his own home, but he could have looked elsewhere for it.

"Walk me through the events of that day," I said.

He nodded. "All right. Sometimes on Sunday, after the guests have gone, and before we welcome new ones on Monday, we have a get together at one of our abodes. We have a few drinks, relax, catch up with each other. I hosted the last one."

"Who was there?"

"Everyone. Everyone who works here, I mean."

"Except me," Grace said. "I was in my office most of the evening, doing some last-minute prepping for the next guests."

"She's right, sorry. I meant to say all the staff was there."

"Who had access to your bedroom?"

"Everyone. You go through my room to get to the bathroom. Seems like everyone used it at some point during the evening."

"Did anyone cut out early or stay longer than the rest?" I asked.

He pondered the question. "Clara left first, and Karl a few minutes after. She seemed upset."

"What was she doing before she left?"

"Talking to Karl."

"About what?"

"I don't know. They were outside on the deck. Abby walked out to join them, and Clara got angry and took off. Karl left a few minutes later."

"Did either of them return?' I asked.

"Karl did."

"How much later?"

"I can't remember. Wasn't long, I don't think. He seemed a little odd when he walked back in, now that I think about it. About an hour later, we all called it a night."

"What time was that?"

"Around nine."

"Seems a bit early, doesn't it?" I asked.

"It's my doing, I'm afraid," Grace said. "I always want them to be refreshed for the arrival of the new guests, so I remind them to wrap things up earlier than later. I never specify a time or check up on them or anything. They respect me, and I respect them."

Turning back to Calvin, I said, "When did you notice the gun was missing?"

"After everyone had gone. I sat there, trying to remember when I saw it last."

"Which was when?" Foley asked.

"It was there on Saturday. Saw it when I opened the drawer for some sleeping pills. On Sunday night, I noticed it was gone. I've been over that evening many times, trying to remember who was coming and going, when and where. Thing is, I may have indulged in a few more drinks than usual. It's all a bit fuzzy."

"What you're saying is, you don't remember anything specific," Foley said.

Calvin shook his head. "Sorry. Wish I did."

"I assume you looked around for the gun outside your own home," Foley said.

"Not as much as I should have, but I did search Clara's place when she wasn't home."

"Why Clara?" I asked.

"I remembered a conversation we'd had weeks a while back. An old boyfriend was trying to get in touch with her, someone from the past, from the days when she was thieving. She didn't trust the guy, and she worried he'd find out where she worked and show up here. I assured her I would keep an eye out, like I always do."

"And what did she say?"

"She said she appreciated it, but she thought she'd feel even more safe if she had a weapon."

"Did you tell her you had one?"

"Of course not. Still, I wondered if she'd seen it that night and decided to take it or borrow it."

"Did anyone else here know you had it?" I asked.

"I don't think so."

"Why bring a gun to the retreat in the first place?" I asked.

"Habit, I guess. I've kept one in my nightstand for as long as I can remember. I was raised in a good neighborhood, with nice houses, the kind of houses thugs like to break into. Ours was hit a couple of times. My dad always kept a gun within reach at night, for protection. He taught me to do the same. And the way I see it, I didn't assault that girl back then no matter what she said. Why should I have to give up the right to carry a firearm because I was falsely accused?"

"Because it's the law," Foley said.

"Yeah, well, the law doesn't always get it right."

"I agree," I said. "They don't."

Foley shook his head at me.

He was not impressed.

"It's the truth," I said to Foley. "We both know it. I mean, look, I'd love to be right all the time, but I've made just as many mistakes as everyone else. And I believe him, Foley. I believe he served time for a crime he didn't commit."

"And now?" Foley asked. "Guess you've decided he had nothing to do with Clara's or Quinn's murders either."

"I want to believe he's telling the truth."

But was he?

If the murderer worked at the retreat, we were down to seven suspects.

Abby.

Kelly.

Rebecca.

Tyler.

Karl.

Grace.

Calvin.

Some I suspected more than others. I needed to flesh out my suspicions, one by one until I figured it all out.

I stood.

"Where do you think you're going?" Foley asked.

"If you want to keep questioning Calvin, go for it. I have others places to be."

"Where?"

"For starters, I need to have a little chat with Karl."

39

I found Karl in the kitchen, foraging around the refrigerator for something to make for dinner. He smiled and said, "Looks like we're on our own tonight. I've just spoken to Tyler. He's not in the mood to cook, or eat, which is understandable, considering the circumstances."

"It doesn't seem to have ruined your appetite," I said.

He set the loaf of bread he was holding on a plate and walked over to me. "I suppose I have a different way of looking at life and death than most people."

"And what way would that be?"

"I don't think about life in terms of beginnings or endings. We're all here for a certain period of time. None of us know how long that is or when we're going to go. To me, what matters is making the most of what we have now, of each day and every moment within that day."

"Are you saying the murders don't bother you? Because to me, deaths like these are perfect examples of people being taken before their time."

"Are *you* bothered?"

"Answer the question," I said

"I don't like the way in which Quinn or Clara died. But the fact is they're at peace now. Whatever troubles they carried in this life won't matter in the next."

"We have no idea what's beyond this life," I said. "How would *you* know if they're at peace or not?"

"When you study creation, our existence, and who we are as it relates to the frequency of the earth and to each other, you tap into something far more elaborate than most people could ever comprehend."

It sounded like gibberish nonsense, a way for him to deflect from the conversation we were having.

"I'm not here to talk about your theories on life," I said.

"What are you here to talk about then? What's *really* troubling you, Georgiana? Because I don't believe it's the fact that I am not taking these deaths as serious as you are."

I knew what was troubling me, and why. "I get the feeling everyone here is keeping things from me."

He crossed his arms and leaned back against the countertop. "I wonder … is that because everyone is keeping things from you? Or is it because you've told yourself they are?"

"What are you talking about?" I asked.

"We lie to ourselves at times, tell stories, create narratives in our minds because we've felt something or thought something, and in order to understand it, we feel the need to put it somewhere. So we create our own truth, which is sometimes a version of the truth, but not the reality of it."

I wanted to say I didn't understand, didn't interpret his meaning, but I did. I supposed there was a shred of truth to his words, and yes, I had told myself everyone was keeping something from me. I was almost certain most of them were.

"We need to talk about Sunday night," I said.

He opened the refrigerator and removed some lunchmeat, cheese, and condiments. "I don't know about you, but I need to eat. Care for a sandwich?"

"I'm fine."

"Suit yourself."

In truth, my stomach had been growling ever since I'd laid eyes on the sourdough bread. But I had bigger problems. Dinner could wait.

As Karl made himself a sandwich, I continued with my questions. "Sunday evening you and the rest of the staff were at Calvin's place."

"That's right."

"Calvin said something seemed to be bothering Clara that night, and she left early. Prior to saying goodnight, she was seen on the deck. One minute she was talking to you; the next, she walked out. You followed a few minutes later."

"We were just having a discussion among friends."

"About what?" I asked.

I could tell by the look on his face he didn't want to elaborate on what they'd talked about. It was the first time his pleasant demeanor had changed, his face turning dour and serious.

"I'd rather not speak ill of the dead," he said. "You know how I feel about that. Clara was a dear friend."

"A dear friend who's dead," I said. "So please, answer my question."

He cut his sandwich in half, sighing as he set it down on a plate. "If I answer your question, I'd like you to let me eat in peace."

"Is this your way of telling me you'd like me to get lost?"

"It's my way of telling you I need some time to myself tonight."

"I understand."

He looked at me with doubt.

"I don't want you to take this the wrong way, but sometimes after I've been in your presence, I feel the need to gather myself and my thoughts. You are different than anyone I've ever experienced before."

"Different how?" I asked.

"That's a question I cannot answer right now. It's something I've been pondering all week."

"You've been pondering about *me* all week?"

"It's more like I've been trying to connect with a frequency that cannot connect." We were both quiet for a moment, then he added, "I'm sorry. I shouldn't say things like that to you. It's not right. No matter what the journey has been this week, it doesn't change my dedication to you and your well-being."

"Maybe you should have been straight with me. Maybe it's what you should have done all along."

He poured himself a glass of water and then another for me. He set mine in front of me on the counter, took a few sips of his, and said, "It's not often I meet a person who seems so connected and disconnected to herself at the same time."

"What do you mean?"

"I get the feeling you have a hard time letting those close to you into your life, letting them see the inner layers of the seasoned onion, the ones that aren't always the prettiest parts to see. You shouldn't hide parts of yourself from those you love. If they love you in return, they'll accept you, blemishes and all."

Why did it seem like every time I tried talking to this guy, we ended up sidetracked down a road I never wanted to be on?

"My onion is complex," I said. "I get it. But I'd like to get back to what happened to Clara on Sunday night."

He nodded. "I was out on the deck, alone, taking a moment to enjoy the night sky. Clara joined me, and it didn't take long for me to see she was upset."

"Over what?"

"She'd seen me with Abby engaged in a way that led her to believe we were more than friends."

"Why did she care about you and Abby?"

"Some time ago, Clara mistook my compassion and kindness as romantic feelings. At the end of one of our sessions, she hugged me.

It seemed innocent enough. I don't find hugging to be inappropriate. It was after the hug when it became a problem. She tried to kiss me."

"What did you do?"

"My concern, first and foremost, was not to embarrass her. The fact that she mistook my feelings of friendship as something more wasn't her fault. Nor was it mine. It was a simple, innocent misunderstanding. I explained this to her in a way she seemed to understand, and it never happened again."

"How long ago was this?" I asked.

"Several months now."

"And how did she behave toward you after the misunderstanding?"

"Timid and a bit standoffish at first, but over time, we started getting back to the way things were."

"When she saw you with Abby, was she angry over what she witnessed because you'd rejected her, but you didn't reject Abby?"

"I believe it was a combination of the two. When I told Clara I liked her as a friend, I believe she took it to mean the same friendship extended to all coworkers, and it does not."

"So, she left Calvin's party, and you went after her?"

"I did. I wanted to make sure she was all right."

"And was she?"

"Not at first, but I remained by her side until she calmed down."

"When you were at Calvin's place, did you notice anything out of the ordinary?"

He shook his head.

"Were you ever in his bedroom or bathroom?" I asked.

"I use the lavatory right after I returned from consoling Clara."

"Did you happen to notice anything out of place in his bedroom, or if his nightstand drawer was open?"

"It was closed. I think I would have remembered if it was hanging open."

My phone vibrated in my pocket. I picked it up, looked at the Caller ID. It was Hunter. Earlier in the day, she'd told Simone there was something she'd found out. Something important. And in the craziness of the day's events, I'd forgotten all about it.

40

I'm sorry, Hunter," I said. "It's been a madhouse around here."

"It's fine," Hunter said. "Simone just called me. She let me know about Clara. What do you think of the suicide note?"

"If it was Clara's handwriting, I believe it was done so under duress."

"You think someone forced her to write it?"

"I do."

"Why would she?"

"People do a lot of things when there's a gun pointed at them," I said. "I've been thinking a lot about the time I spent with Clara this morning. Nothing in her demeanor makes me think she was contemplating suicide."

"Let's say you're right and someone else shot her. How is her death connected to Quinn's?"

"I'm guessing Quinn found out something she shouldn't have, and she died because of it."

There was a pause, and then she said, "I may be able to help you there. When Quinn owned the flower shop, she'd drive home to visit her mother from time to time. One of those times, she'd stopped to pick up something at the store, and along the way, her purse tipped over, spilling all the contents at her feet. A pill bottle rolled beneath the gas pedal, and she panicked. She reached down to grab it and didn't see a little boy chasing after his dog in the street."

Every possible scenario of what happened next ran through my mind.

None of the scenarios were good.

"Please don't say she ran the boy over," I said.

"She did."

"Did he survive?"

"His name was Lucas Parker. He was in a coma for a couple months. But yeah, he died."

"What are his parents' names?"

"Lori and Casey Parker."

"I'm assuming that's when Quinn closed the flower shop."

"I'd say so. She was arrested for manslaughter. People in town were divided about their feelings, but a lot of them believed she deserved to be behind bars."

"Did she serve time?" I asked.

"Because of the nature of the accident, and the fact she couldn't drive with all the contents from her bag rolling around, the court was lenient. Quinn was sentenced to probation, her license was suspended for a while, she was given a steep fine, and she served around a thousand hours of community service."

"And how did the boys' parents react to the verdict?"

"Here's where it gets even worse. Not long after his death, the boy's mother shot herself in the head."

Shot herself in the head, just like Quinn had been shot in the head.

Revenge seemed to have been exacted, but by whom?

"What about the father?" I asked.

"He's still alive, living in the same house in Cambria too. When you didn't call me back, I gave his information to Simone. She was supposed to call him."

"Did the boy have any siblings?"

"I don't believe so, but I'll find out."

It was a lot to take in.

I did a quick recap of the events as we knew them.

While visiting her mother in Cambria, Quinn hit a boy, putting him into a coma, which led to his death. Traumatized over the accident, she closed the flower shop. Then she was arrested for manslaughter. At trial, the court decides the boy's death was a horrific accident. In lieu of prison time, they slapped her on the wrist with fines and community service and sent her on her way.

I could understand how it didn't sit well with some town residents.

"What happened after the trial was over?" I asked.

"Quinn started receiving hate mail. She even received a few death threats from people who didn't feel the punishment matched the crime."

"What happened to that kid was awful. But it could happen to any of us, at any time."

"I know, but they were grieving. They needed someone to blame."

"What did she do after serving her community service?"

"She moved. I'm guessing she wanted to start over in a town where people didn't know her. Within three months, she got married, changed her first and last names, and got pregnant."

Quinn had a new life, a new husband, and a baby on the way. But inside, she knew who she was, and she knew what she'd done. There was no escaping it. The pain of that day haunted her for the rest of her life.

It was no coincidence that she ended up at the retreat.

No coincidence she'd died the way she had.

And now I just needed to figure out who still had an axe to grind.

41

Before we ended the call, I asked Hunter to put a file together on every staff member at the retreat. I wanted to know what they were doing the year Quinn ran over the Parker boy. I wanted photos, the addresses of where they lived and worked back then—anything she could find. I also wanted to know where Clara had been living in recent years, and if there was a possibility the story in the note had any truth to it.

In the meantime, I had some snooping of my own to do.

I passed by Foley undetected. He was in Grace's office, still conversing with her and Calvin. Man, the guy was longwinded sometimes. Silas and a couple other officers were still collecting evidence in Clara's room, which freed me up to do a bit of digging around at Calvin's residence before the police picked it apart.

I stepped up to Calvin's front porch and my phone buzzed.

It was Faith.

"How are you doing?" I asked.

"Not good," she sniffled. "The cops were here a while ago. They told me some things that I … well, I just don't understand. And when I tried to get them to explain, they wouldn't say much of anything. I was hoping you could answer a few questions for me."

I had some questions for her too.

"Sure, what do you want to know?" I asked.

"Why did they ask me if I knew someone had broken into my mother's house?"

"In one of her sessions with Karl, your mother said her house had been broken into. There was a message left on the bathroom mirror in lipstick."

"What message?"

"It said: I know who you are, and I know what you did."

"I … I can't believe it. Why didn't she say anything to me? I don't understand."

"Maybe she didn't want you to worry, and she thought it was better not to say anything. Given you're in your first trimester of pregnancy, I can't say I blame her. It's a sensitive time. Anything could happen, and my guess is your mom was looking out for you and the baby."

"The cops said something about another death at the retreat. What happened?"

Her tone expressed concern, but was it genuine … or not?

I wasn't sure.

"Earlier today, Clara was found dead inside her room," I said. "She died of a gunshot wound. When I found her, she wasn't alone. She was with Tyler."

"The chef?"

"Yep. He claimed they were supposed to go for a walk. And that's not all. We found a suicide note on the counter. It's possible she wrote it."

"What did the note say?"

"She confessed to killing your mother."

"What? Why did she say she did it?"

"According to the note, your mother wouldn't give Clara a job. She had just gotten out of jail, and your mom felt like she couldn't trust her. It upset Clara to the point that she couldn't let it go."

A pause and then, "Doesn't sound like something my mom would say or do. If anything, she's sympathetic to people who've had a rough go in life. Seems kinda lame to shoot a person for not giving you a job, doesn't it?"

"I agree," I said. "I'm suspicious of the note."

"Suspicious how?"

"I'm just not buying the explanation."

"If Clara didn't kill my mother, then who did?"

Someone who had real motive.

Someone who knew Quinn's secret.

"I'm still trying to find answers," I said. "I will. I just need time. For now, I have some questions for you, if you don't mind."

"Yeah, sure."

"Before you were born, your mother owned a flower shop, and she went by a different name. Brynn. What do you know about that?"

"Not much. I doubt she would have mentioned it to me except I found an old driver's license of hers inside a zippered compartment of a suitcase she hadn't used in years. I asked her about it, and all she said was she never liked the name Brynn, so when she married my dad, she changed it."

"Did it ever come up again?"

"Not with her, but while I was living with my dad, I asked him."

"What did he say?"

"He told me some things are better left in the past. I've always known something happened to my mom before I was born, something bad. Her bouts of depression were hard, and even though my dad tried to be patient with her, it upset him that she didn't try harder to move on. Maybe if she had, they would have stayed married."

I thought about telling her what I had learned about her mother's car accident and about the boy. She deserved to know. But maybe tonight wasn't the right time.

"The night your mother died, she was thinking of leaving the retreat and heading home," I said. "She'd even called a friend to come pick her up, but in the end, she decided to stay. Do you know what changed her mind?"

There was another pause, a pause that lasted so long, it made me question whether she was still on the line, even though I had no reason to believe she'd disconnected.

"Faith, you still there?" I asked.

More sniffling sounds and then, "Yeah, I know why she wanted to leave. It was all my fault."

"What was your fault?"

"It was my fault she wanted to leave. She came to talk to me that night, and I know that I should have listened to what she had to say, but I was so drained already from our first couple of days together, I didn't know how much more of her emotions I could take. I shut her down before she could get much out. I felt awful about it. I'd promised to be there for her, to help her through it all, and I wasn't. I didn't know she was going to be so hard to handle—or that confronting the past would consume her like it did. I didn't know how to deal with it."

"I'm sure you tried your best."

"I wish I could take it back, could have listened to her, and been there when she needed me."

I wanted to reach through the phone and hug her. It was clear she needed it.

"Your mother wouldn't want you to feel this way," I said.

"It's just hard, you know? You never think when you lash out at someone that it's going to be the last time you ever see them. That morning when I knocked at her door, ready to go on our morning walk, I was in a better headspace. I wanted to make everything right. I had no idea I'd never get the chance."

She began to weep.

She was no killer.

She just wasn't.

I gave her a moment and tried to think about what I could say to bring her comfort. "Your mother would want you to be happy, Faith. She'd want you to live your best life and find the happiness that she never could. If there's one thing you can do for her now, it would be to remember the good things, the fond memories you have that you can pass on to your child. I believe she'd want that for you both."

"I'll try. It's just sad, you know? She drove me crazy at times, but I miss her. I miss her so much."

I thought of my relationship with my own mother. If I could describe the dynamic between us, I guess it was like a rubber band. Even when I distanced myself a little bit, I always felt myself snapping back, wanting her approval and her affection, even though it was hard to admit. If there was a lesson for me to learn from all this, it was to appreciate the role my mother played in my life, and to be grateful she was here. Not everyone had that.

"I'd better run, Faith," I said. "I'm so glad you called."

"Yeah, me too."

"Before I go, I was wondering what you could tell me about Jane. What kind of friend was she to your mother? When did they meet?"

"Jane's a good friend, someone my mom could lean on. She's always been there for her. Why do you ask?"

"I'd like to speak with Jane," I said. "Do you have her phone number?"

"I do, just a second." There was a pause and then she returned to the line giving me Jane's details. We said our goodbyes, and as soon as I ended the call, I looked up and saw Calvin heading my way. His arms were crossed, eyes inquisitive, like he wondered what I was doing on his doorstep.

It seemed my window of opportunity to search his place was gone.

42

Part of me wanted to keep going all night, but given the late hour, my aching body had other ideas. After the day we'd just had, I was exhausted. I decided to stay in, get some rest, and start fresh in the morning.

After a long soak in the bathtub, I slipped into bed and called Giovanni to check in. When the call was over, Simone entered the room. Thinking we'd spend some time talking about the case before we went to sleep, she'd made herself a strong cup of tea. She was talking so fast I struggled to keep up.

She plopped down next to me and told me about the phone call she'd had with Casey Parker. More like *tried* to have. Casey was disinterested in dredging up the past and refused to talk about what happened all those years ago. What's more, he was happy to hear Quinn was dead.

In his words, justice had been served at long last.

After we discussed the short phone call, I suggested she sleep in her own bungalow tonight. She shot the idea down, which I expected.

I was starting to miss the time I'd had to myself at the start of the week. I didn't consider myself cohabitating material, even though Giovanni and I were making it work. He always seemed to know what I needed, and we respected one another's space, which made coexisting in the same house a lot easier. He wasn't always around either. He often jetted off somewhere, doing something for the family business. It gave me time to recharge my battery.

Thinking of him now, and of Luka, I wanted nothing more than to return home to my man and my pooch. I needed this case to be over, but if I wanted to close it, I needed answers I still didn't have. For now, it was tomorrow's problem.

Sleep came fast, and I went the entire night without waking.

While Simone showered the next morning, I called Quinn's friend Jane. She wasted no time shedding light on the woman Quinn was post-car accident, a woman forever changed, forever trying to get her life back. Jane reminisced on the good times and bad, the moments where Quinn showed the slightest glimmer of the fun-loving woman she was before Lucas Parker's death.

When I mentioned the message left in lipstick in Quinn's home, I was surprised to learn Jane knew about it. She'd begged Quinn to go to the police. Quinn refused. Involving the police meant she'd have to explain who she was and unpack a past she was still too embarrassed to admit—especially to authorities.

Quinn believed the message was nothing more than an idle threat written by someone who wanted her to know she'd been found. A scare tactic intended to rile her. She didn't believe she was in real danger, or if she did, she wouldn't admit it to anyone.

Jane disagreed with Quinn's decision to do nothing but found a satisfying compromise. She'd keep quiet *if* Quinn agreed to install security cameras at the front and back of her house and give Jane access to monitor the feed through her cell phone. If the intruder returned, they'd both know about it.

A second break-in never happened.

As to who was behind the threat, Quinn claimed she didn't know. She hadn't kept any of the letters she'd received after the boy's death, and she hadn't turned them over to police either. She'd burned them, destroying any chance we had to connect them to her murderer.

Maybe Quinn had assumed that after so much time had passed, she'd been all but forgotten. But for one person, Quinn was still very much at the forefront of their mind.

43

The sharp sting of winter's morning air felt different today somehow. It whistled through the trees, bending and twisting—restless, like it sensed today would be different.

Perhaps it would be.

Perhaps today the answers I'd been seeking would come.

Justice would be served.

It was nice to think of the day ending with me looking the killer in the eye, ushering in the day of reckoning.

I was outside on the back deck with my robe wrapped around me. As my thoughts wandered, I glanced over to the porch next to mine. Quinn's porch. If she were still alive, maybe we would have been outside together at this very moment, swapping stories over our first cup of coffee of the day. The mere thought of it sent a chill through me, or maybe it was the frigidity of the air. I wasn't sure.

It was half past six in the morning, and I'd already been awake for an hour. Ever since I was a child, I'd been an early riser. There was a sense of stillness and calm in the morning hours, something I didn't get any other way.

I took a sip of coffee and noticed Grace shuffling toward me. She seemed a bit disoriented this morning, unlike her usual serene, collected self.

She bent over the wood railing and blew out a long sigh.

"Is everything okay?" I asked.

She shook her head. "I didn't sleep much last night, which is unusual for me."

"It seems normal, given what's going on right now."

"It's not normal for me," she said. "It's not often I have a problem coming to terms with things in life, even hard things, like losing Clara."

"You're not alone. Everyone is rattled over what happened yesterday."

She nodded and said, "Clara stopped by my office the other day. At the time, I was in a meeting with Abby. She kept pacing outside. It was obvious something was bothering her. Whenever she got nervous, she bit down on her nails. Bit them to the nubs sometimes."

"What did you do when you saw her?" I asked.

"Not what I should have done. Instead of excusing myself from the conversation with Abby, I asked her to come back later."

"What was it about your conversation with Abby that couldn't wait?"

"It wasn't that it couldn't wait. I was used to Clara coming to me whenever she was having a bad day. She could be sensitive at times and would become agitated over the smallest things. I thought that's all it was—Clara making more of something than was necessary. I figured once I finished with Abby, Clara and I could talk, and I'd help her get past whatever she was going through, just like I always did."

"Did you speak to her later?" I asked.

"I tried. She blew me off, and I'm guessing it's because she felt I'd blown her off."

"You did blow her off."

"I know. And now I keep wondering if not making her a priority led her to … you know, killing herself. I expect that's why I was up most of the night. It's been many years since I've allowed the guilt of my actions to creep in. It's not a good feeling."

I finished my cup of coffee, set it to the side, and crossed one leg over the other. "I'm no mental health genius, but maybe what you felt is you being real with yourself for once. Maybe you felt a kind of realness you haven't allowed yourself to feel because you don't like how you feel when you do. I imagine you'd rather stay in your perfect bubble of happiness and bliss. That's not life though. Real life isn't fake or fashioned. It's allowing yourself to become raw and real, to feel emotions, whether you want to or not."

She thought about what I'd said for a time and then nodded. "I do believe I've learned something from *you* today. You're a lot more in touch with yourself than you give yourself credit for, you know."

I'd never been comfortable with compliments, making this the perfect time to segue the conversation back to the one we were having before.

"I'm not so sure Clara committed suicide," I said.

"Why would you question it after the note she left?"

"I just am. I'm not sure why yet. From what you've said about her and what little time we spent together, it's obvious she was moody. But it seemed like she acted out because she wanted attention."

"I agree with you there. I felt the same way about her."

"Let's say there was no note. Would you still think Clara committed suicide?"

She considered the question. "I haven't thought of it that way. I'm of two minds, I suppose. Given her personality, I'd say she was capable of such a thing. But when I think about how hard she was trying to build a new life for herself, it makes me think twice."

"What about murder? Do you think she was capable of it?"

"I would say it depended on the person. That ex-boyfriend of hers, the one she was worried about … I think she would have done anything to keep him out of her life."

"What do you know about him?" I asked.

"He's back in jail again. Has been for a couple of weeks."

A couple of weeks meant there was no connection between him and what had gone on at the retreat.

"Have you seen the suicide note?" I asked.

"I have. Chief Foley showed it to me last night, asked me if I recognized the handwriting. Looked like hers, but I'm no expert."

"It just feels like I'm missing something."

"Something like what?"

"Motive, for one. The one offered in the note was almost laughable, even for someone as sensitive as Clara. Plus, I don't believe it's the reason Quinn was murdered."

"What do you mean?"

"When Quinn arrived here, she was carrying the heavy weight of something that happened in her past. Something I feel she was working on getting up the courage to talk to Karl about before she left here. I believe someone was seeking revenge, and that's why she was murdered."

"Do you know what happened in her past?"

"I do now," I said.

"Is it something you can share?"

"Not yet."

"If it happened some time ago, why wouldn't the person holding the grudge go after her right after the incident? Why wait so long to confront her?"

It was another question I wasn't prepared to answer, but I didn't blame her for asking. If I didn't already know the answer, I would be thinking the same thing.

"There are a lot of things I'm still trying to work out," I said. "Until I do, I'm not satisfied with closing the case yet."

She moved her hands to her hips. "Whatever you've discovered about Quinn, it must be big. I hope it won't take long for you to find the answers. I have no doubt you will. Is there anything I can do to help?"

"Not right now. I'll let you know if anything comes up."

She lifted a finger and said, "Ahh, I almost forgot the reason I came to speak with you in the first place. Tyler quit this morning, which means he won't be making breakfast—or anything else for that matter. I'm heading over to the kitchen now to see what I can whip up. I apologize things are such a mess right now."

"You don't need to bother cooking for us. We have no problem making something ourselves."

"I appreciate that, but I need to make sure any remaining staffers are fed as well. I don't need anyone else quitting on me. Shall we say nine o'clock?"

"Works for me. Listen, I've been meaning to ask you, did you know Abby and Karl have been having sex?"

She grinned. "I do catch wind of things now and then."

It wasn't a straight answer, and I could tell I'd caught her off-guard.

"It seems Clara made an advance toward Karl as well," I said. "He refused her, and then she caught him and Abby in a precarious position together. I believe it's the reason Clara left Calvin's place on Sunday night. She was upset."

"Clara made a pass at Karl? I'm surprised to hear you say that. I can't believe it's true."

"Why not?"

"It's just, I was under the impression that Clara had started to prefer ... well, women."

44

Clara may have *liked* women, but she had an ex-boyfriend, which meant she'd dated men in the past. Maybe she had been attracted to both genders.

I walked toward the staff quarters, mulling over the conversation I just had with Grace. Tyler passed by, carrying an overstuffed black trash bag.

"Hey," I said. "You're just the person I was coming to see."

He stopped and turned toward me. "Oh yeah, why?"

"I heard you quit. Is that true?"

"Yep."

He glanced toward the parking lot as if anxious to get to his car.

"Where are you headed now?" I asked.

"Home, I guess."

"Where's home?"

"Here, in Pismo Beach."

Pismo Beach.

A short, one-hour drive from Cambria.

"Is that where your parents live?" I asked.

"Yep."

"I have a few questions for you, but the bag you're carrying looks heavy. I can walk with you to your car if you like."

He looked at the bag, shrugged, and started walking.

It seemed my nosiness with regard to the bag needed to be a bit more direct.

"What's in the bag?" I asked.

"Clothes."

I wanted to wrangle it away from him and rip the bag open. He was skittish. I wondered if it was because of Clara or if it had to do with something else.

"What do you plan on doing for work?" I asked.

"Don't know yet. Haven't given it much thought."

"You just quit, so you gave that some thought."

He closed his eyes, sighed. "Look, I'm not trying to be rude, but I just want to leave. I don't want to be here anymore. Not after … anyway, I just need to go. Okay?"

"Did you love Clara?" I asked.

He popped open the trunk of his Subaru and tossed the bag in. Then he stood for a moment looking at it, as if he'd rather look at it than look at me.

I wasn't leaving until he answered my question.

"You loved her, didn't you?" I asked.

He scrunched up a brow. "What makes you think that?"

"The night Quinn died when Clara asked you to help her keep an eye on me.

Every time I looked at you, you were looking at Clara."

"Doesn't mean I *loved* her. She was all shook up that night. I was just watching out for her."

"Is it possible you loved her, but she didn't love you?"

"We were good friends. Nothing more."

"Grace seems to think Clara liked women in a romantic way," I said. "Do you know anything about that?"

He closed the trunk and leaned against it. "Maybe."

"What about an advance she made toward Karl? Did she ever mention it to you?"

He clenched a fist.

He knew about Karl.

"She showed an interest in Karl," I said. "Didn't she?"

"Yeah, I guess so."

"I bet it would be hard to find out the person you liked had an interest in someone else, someone much older than you. It's natural. Normal, even. Jealousy is a part of life. It's just … I wonder. Jealousy can sometimes be managed. It's when it turns into something more that there's a problem. When jealousy turns to rage, for example."

"What are you talking about?"

"I'm not accusing you of being jealous, and I'm not saying you have issues with rage. From what I've seen, you're quiet but observant. I do wonder if there's another side of you though, and if the man on display for all to see is the man you really are. Or is there someone else beneath the exterior, someone no one else is aware of except for you."

"Not sure what you're trying to say, but I'm done talking."

"I'm not."

He threw his hands in the air and shouted, "What do you want me to say here? Whatever it is, just tell me, and I'll say it just so you'll leave me alone. Do you want me to say I loved her? Fine, I did. And she loved me too. She just couldn't admit it to herself."

"Why couldn't she?"

"Clara was always too caught up in her head all the time, thinking she was damaged goods and only deserved to be with someone who was damaged just like her."

His comment had me thinking.

If she pursued people who were damaged, why did she pursue Karl?

I was sure Karl had another side to him too.

Everyone did.

Tyler bit down on his lip, and for a moment, I thought he was about to get emotional. He breathed out a few times, settling himself, and then said, "I didn't kill her, and that's all you need to know."

"Thank you," I said.

"For what?"

"Answering my questions. Well, most of them. You still haven't told me your thoughts on whether Clara dated both men and women."

"Why does it matter?"

"I don't know that it does. I'm just trying to piece it all together, and to do that, it helps me to know as much as I can about the person."

"We didn't talk a lot about it, but one night, after a few drinks, she made a comment that made me think she went both ways." He pushed himself off the back of the car and reached into his pocket, pulling out his car keys. "I'd like to go now."

"Before you do, I have one more question. Every time I see you, you're always fiddling around with the beaded bracelet on your wrist. It's almost like messing with it calms your nerves. I get it. I have ways of calming my nerves too."

"What about it?"

"Where did you get the bracelet?"

A long pause, and then, "I'd rather not say."

"Why?"

"Old memories."

Painful ones, no doubt.

"Did you make the bracelet yourself, or did someone make it for you?"

"It was given to me."

"Is the person who gave it to you the reason you don't want to talk about it? Is this person no longer in your life?"

"Something like that. I'm not talking about it, okay?"

He grabbed the door handle and got in, starting the car and then backing away, leaving me standing there, thinking about the bracelet, and about him.

Had a man given it to him or a woman?

Or was it a child … a child who was no longer living?

45

hat did you say?" I asked through the phone. "Silas? I can't hear you. You're going to have to turn the music down."

"Oh, sorry," he shouted. "Hold tight."

I heard footsteps. The music got louder at first. Then it went quiet.

"Can you hear me now?" he asked.

"I can. Who's the band? They sound a lot more modern than some of the big-hair bands you listen to at the lab."

"They're called Maneskin. Great band. Saw them in New York City last month."

Their music was right up my alley. "I'll check them out."

"You should. You'll dig their stuff."

"When I answered the phone, it sounded like you were trying to tell me something about the case."

"Yeah, so the hair fibers I pulled off the clothing Quinn wore on the night she died were cat hairs," Silas said.

"Let me guess, a black cat?"

"How'd you know?"

"There is a black cat that roams the property. She belongs to Abby."

"What do you know about her?"

"She was in jail for a bar fight, and it wasn't her first. She's also been involved in a romantic relationship with one of the other employees here."

"Is there anything about her that would suggest she's behind the murders?"

"I don't know of any reason she'd have to kill Quinn," I said. "But there was a weird love triangle going on between Abby, Clara, and Karl."

"Wait, wait. Karl the old dude?"

"Yeah, it seems he's a hot commodity around this place. I can't figure out why. The guy's strange. I don't find him attractive in the least."

"There's, what, three guys working out there with a bunch of single women? People aren't as picky when there isn't much choice. I suppose there's someone for everyone, just like the saying goes, right?"

"I guess. What can you tell me about Clara? Have you been able to examine her body in more detail yet?"

"Still early days. The position of the body was all wrong for a person who shot herself. The trajectory of the blood spatter would suggest the gun was fired at a farther range than Clara would have been able to achieve herself. As far as it being a suicide, I'm not feeling it—or seeing proof of it, for that matter."

"I agree. What about the suicide note?"

"We found a few samples of writing in Clara's desk drawer. We're running a comparison between those samples and the note. When it comes to things like this, it's important to look at what she said and how she said it."

"How she phrased some of the things she said has been bugging me. I just can't figure out why."

"I have no doubt you will," he said. "As far as suspects go, you feeling anyone more than the others?"

"I've thought about each one of them so many times I'm starting to overthink, to create motives in my head, for each of them. In every scenario I create, there is a plausible reason for them to commit murder. I feel like I need to take a step back, to rethink what I know about the case since it started."

He laughed. "Ahh, so you're saying we need to have one of our usual talks then."

"I'm not sure I'm in the frame of mind to do that right now."

"Why not? They're so much fun."

"Fun for you, maybe."

He was laughing a lot harder now. "What's not fun about unloading what's on your mind?"

"I don't know where to begin this time. I can't even find a connection between Quinn's murder and Clara's."

"Tell you what, give me a couple of hours to process some things I'm working on, and then I'll call you back. Want my advice? Clear your mind. Think about each person as an individual. You're amazing at recalling the kind of clues others don't see, things that don't seem out of the ordinary, but lead you to solve the case in the end. Don't think in hypotheticals. Think in *fact* and in *truth* and see what comes to you."

He was right.

The truth was right in front of me.

I could feel it.

I just needed to see it.

46

I thought about going to talk to Abby, to ask her about the cat hair found on Quinn's clothing the night she died. But before I did that, I needed some alone time. I decided the best way to reconnect was to take a walk.

What had started as a gloomy, bleak day, had turned out to be a pleasant one. The sun was out, and as I walked, its rays penetrated my skin, and I felt a sense of renewal—and with it, clarity.

As far as suspects went, I'd narrowed it down to a few, my gut instincts believing the man or woman I was looking for was someone associated with the retreat.

Take Grace herself, a woman determined to turn people's lives around. A woman who was her name personified. She seemed kind and caring, and when it came to Clara's death, her emotions seemed genuine.

But were they?

Then there was Abby, the caretaker of a black cat. Did the fact that cat hair was found on Quinn's clothing have any meaning, or had Quinn encountered the cat at some point during her stay? Perhaps even allowing the cat into her place.

There was the love triangle between Karl, Abby, and Clara, which wasn't much of a love triangle at all. It seemed to be more of a misunderstanding than anything else.

But was it?

The arson sisters, Rebecca and Kelly, had never given me a reason to suspect them, and I'd all but ruled them out. They had no motive, and unlike the subtle clues I'd discovered with a few of the others, there was nothing leading me to believe they were involved with either murder.

Next, we had Tyler, a man who couldn't seem to remove his hand from his homemade bracelet. What was the significance of the bracelet? Who had given it to him? And why did he struggle to talk about it? When he learned of Clara's interest in Karl, could hidden rage have gotten the better of him?

This led me to another interesting theory—that I wasn't looking for just one murderer, but two. I imagined a scenario where Tyler killed Clara, knowing there was already one homicide being investigated, and figured he could get away with it by saying Clara killed Quinn, and in her distress, she killed herself.

As far as theories go, it wasn't a bad one.

It wasn't a good one either.

It was far too complex.

We were dealing with someone who was one step ahead of me, not two.

Plus, Tyler was gaunt. He looked like he'd topple over if someone poked him.

I thought about Karl, the man who presented himself at every turn as a person in complete control, no matter the situation. A man who never let you look under the hood. He knew things about me, but what did I know about him?

Little.

Little of his past, little of his present.

He was sleeping with Abby, in a casual way, but even if that caused a stir in Clara, it didn't mean he had any reason to kill her for it. There was, however, something else. For everything he'd told me about his sessions with Quinn, I was sure there were things she'd said to him that he hadn't shared.

Was it possible something about her past triggered him in some way?

And last, we had Calvin, the security officer, someone whom I wanted to be innocent most of all. In my stubbornness, I'd refused to believe he might be guilty of murder, but had I overlooked something? Take the playing card he used as a bookmark. I couldn't ignore it, couldn't pretend it wasn't possible the cards had meaning of some kind.

As my walk came to an end, it felt like I was nowhere and somewhere at the same time. I took a seat on a bench positioned beneath a shade tree, and my phone buzzed.

Simone had sent me a text message.

Hunter was at the front gate, dropping off the files I had asked her to create on all staff members who worked at the retreat. Simone was on her way down to get them. Maybe after I perused the files, I'd have more answers.

Another text came through from Simone seconds later, this one far more worrisome. When she'd grabbed her bag on the way out the door of my bungalow, her gun wasn't in it. She worried someone had nicked it, slipping in and out of my place without her noticing they were there.

Time was not on our side.

Knowing the walk would take Simone another ten minutes or so I leaned back and breathed in a lungful of fresh air, focusing on my surroundings, every crack, buzz, and inflection.

I made it back to my place and went through it to ensure I was alone. Hunter's files were on the bed, and Simone had left a note saying she was going to check her room—just to confirm she hadn't left her gun there.

I thumbed through the files and then removed my phone from my pocket. I flipped through some of the pictures I'd taken at Clara's place the day before. The suicide note was still on my mind, like a leaky faucet, drip, drip, dripping.

I couldn't shut it off until I resolved whatever problem I seemed to be having with it.

I located the suicide note and read through it.

Once.

Then twice.

And a third time.

There was one particular line that stood out more than the others. Looking at it now, I realized what had been vexing me. In this moment, I was vexed no more. Clara had left me a message—a message about her murderer.

47

oing somewhere?" I asked.

Grace looked up at me and smiled. "Whatever do you mean?"

"I noticed a couple of bags in the back seat of your car just now as I passed by it. Bags that weren't there earlier when I was in the parking lot talking to Tyler. Care to explain?"

"There's nothing *to* explain. Sometimes I'm here later than usual, and I like to bring extra clothes in case I want to change, freshen up. Once a week, I take them home."

Clothing.

I wasn't buying it.

"Open your desk drawers," I said.

"Why?"

"Open them."

"There's nothing to see."

"Then you won't mind showing me."

"What are you getting at, Georgiana? Are you feeling all right?"

"Better than ever. I bet you're not, though."

"Whatever it is you feel you need to say, why not just say it? Let's skip right to the heart of it, shall we?"

"It's not what I need to say to you. It's what you need to say to me. Looks like you're getting ready to leave. Why?"

She shrugged. "I figured since it was so quiet here, I'd head home. No sense sticking around when there aren't any guests left who need anything from me for the remainder of the day. I've called a caterer to bring dinner tonight. Now, if you'll excuse me ..."

"You're not going anywhere," I said.

"Who are you to tell me where I can and cannot go?"

"I'm the person you hired. Remember? And hey, here's a question. The first few times I was in your office, you had a picture on your shelf of two young girls, arm in arm. It's not there now. Where is it?"

Grace swished a hand through the air. "It fell off the shelf and the glass shattered. I haven't had the chance to replace it with everything going on around here."

"But it didn't shatter. Did it? After our conversation this morning, you were worried I'd figure out who the two girls in the photo are. After all, I admitted I knew Quinn's secret. When I first looked at the photo, it was obvious it was dated. I assumed the girls may have been you and your sister when you were younger. I've just been through a handful of files Hunter dropped off. They include details on your history. You don't have a sister. Who's the girl in the photo, Grace?"

"An old childhood friend."

"An old childhood friend who killed herself, isn't that right?"

She glared at me.

I glared back.

She huffed a sigh. "You're right, she's dead. I wouldn't call cancer *killing herself*. She had no control over it."

"Cut the crap, Grace. She didn't die of cancer. She died of a broken heart."

"I don't know what you're talking about."

"Sure, you do. I'll bet the girl in that photo is Lori Parker, mother of Lucas Parker, the boy who was struck by a car by a woman who used to go by the name of Brynn. You must have spent years looking for her. When did you find her?"

"I don't know anyone named Brynn."

"Oh, but you do. What you didn't know was that she'd changed her name all those years ago. At some point you figured it out though, didn't you?"

She shook her head. "And here I thought you were this amazing detective. It would appear you have no one to blame for the murders, so you're blaming me. Why is that? Is it a self-esteem thing? You can't go home without solving it, can you? What I'd like to know is what's really going on. Talk to me."

I was a few seconds away from slapping the woman across her condescending face. She needed to be extracted from her invisible throne, and I knew just how to do it.

"I get a lot of things wrong," I said. "Sometimes I even accuse the wrong person when I'm working a case. But there's one thing I never get wrong—the final clue, the one that ties it all together."

"And what clue would that be?"

"It was the suicide note. Did you read it after you had Clara write it, or did you assume she'd written it just as you'd asked her to do? On second thought, I'm not looking for an answer. There was one thing in the note. One thing she placed just so, hoping one day she'd be vindicated of her confession of murder. Guess what day today is, Grace?"

"What are you talking about?"

"Toward the end of the note, there was a curious sentence, something that I couldn't stop thinking about after I read it. A line that says, 'It's a genuine regret, a careless error on my part.' Seems like a strange thing to say."

"She felt guilty after the murder. She knew she'd made a mistake, and there was no way for her to take it back. It was a careless mistake, and I'm just sorry she made it."

"Except she didn't make a mistake ... *you did*."

"I don't follow."

"The sentence was so odd, I started toying with the words and letters in my mind. I'll read the sentence again: 'It's a genuine regret, a careless error on my part.' Remove some of the words at the beginning and end of that sentence and you're left with 'genuine regret ... a careless error.' Now focus on the first letter in each of those words."

G for Genuine
R for Regret
A for a
C for Careless
E for Error

Her face went white.

I continued.

"Now look at the first word in that sentence: 'It's.' Take out the 'a' after it, and what's left? It's Grace."

48

The moment the revelation came, Grace shot out of her desk chair, pointing an all too familiar gun at me. My gun was aimed at her in turn.

"Simone will be expecting that back," I said.

"And she can have it, *after* I'm done."

"I'm not sure what you think is going to happen here, Grace. But I can tell you this, I'm an excellent shot. If you care to test me, go ahead."

"What does it matter now? Seems I can't find my way out of this, no matter how hard I try."

"You're right. The least you can do is tell me why you did it. I have my suspicions, but hey, if you're going to shoot me, you owe me that much."

Hands shaking, she readjusted her grip on the gun. "Lori Parker and I had been best friends since kindergarten, back when I was shy and quiet and afraid of the world and everything in it. It was Lori who brought me out of my shell. Lori who taught me not to be afraid of life, to embrace it, to accept it. And I did."

"You did until you didn't."

"You don't understand. Quinn didn't just take my godson from me. She took Lori. When he died, she died along with him."

"And you spent all these years trying to find her so you could exact revenge?"

"I tried to move past it, but then something would always happen, a moment I wanted to share with Lori but couldn't—because she was dead. So I'd search again, not knowing what I would do or how it would feel if I found her."

"And then you did, and you broke into her home to leave a message. But the message wasn't enough, was it? She'd moved on, lived her life, while your friend's life was cut short. Must have driven you crazy. You portray yourself as a person who's so much more enlightened than the rest of us, and you're not. You're a hypocrite."

"You're wrong."

"I'm right. You're a fixer. At the end of the day, you wanted to fix everyone.

But there was one person you couldn't fix. You couldn't fix yourself, could you?"

"My desire to help every single woman who's ever come to the retreat to make a better life for themselves has always been genuine."

"Every woman except one," I said.

"I am the same person you thought I was before now. You've seen my employees. You've interacted with them. They're different people now. Better people. And it's all because of me."

"Or is it all because of Karl, and you're taking all the credit?"

She shook a fist at me. "I'm serious about helping people. This place, it means everything to me. My employees served their time for the crimes they committed. They all deserve a fresh start. Quinn didn't spend a single night in a jail cell after the trial ended. Where's the justice in that?"

"Is that why you killed her, to exact justice?" I asked.

"I gave her the sentence she's always deserved. Sometimes the law fails you. When it does, you must take things into your own hands."

She was delusional.

"Was it always your plan to kill Clara?" I asked.

"I never meant to harm a hair on that precious woman's head."

"So why did you?"

"I thought I had everything figured out. A way to kill Quinn, dispose of the murder weapon. It seemed like a good plan. I even expected I could fool you. But here you are."

"Yes, here I am," I said. "Who's the fool now?"

"You're the fool if you're dead."

As gunfire was exchanged, Karl sprinted into the room, throwing himself in front of me. In doing so, he caught the bullet that was meant for me—but Grace would have missed me anyway.

Her aim was as sad as her soul.

My aim on the other hand was spot on.

Grace collapsed to the ground next to Karl.

Moments later, Foley rushed in, his officers behind him.

The moment I'd figured it all out, I'd called him. He'd done what I expected he'd do and asked me to wait to speak to Grace until he arrived. And I'd done what he expected from me, confronting her before she had the chance to flee.

Grace murdered Quinn and Clara, but she left many unanswered questions.

Questions that I still needed to be resolved.

49

K arl had a significant chest wound, but he would survive, as would Grace, which satisfied me. I was certain she'd be convicted and spend the remainder of her life behind bars, which is what she deserved—not just for killing Quinn and Clara— but also for attacking my mother.

Over the next several days, more details emerged as Grace made a full confession. After Lori Parker's suicide, Grace was angry, and she needed somewhere to channel the uncontrollable amount of rage she was carrying around. She started attending spiritual retreats, thinking if she immersed herself in them, she could find a way to move past the loss of her best friend and godson.

It worked for a while, and then the past came flooding back, and Grace would find herself thinking about Lori, the one person she needed most in life. And the anger she'd worked so hard to suppress would creep its way back in, and she'd start searching for Quinn again.

It took many years, but in the end, Grace found Quinn in the simplest of ways. Quinn had returned home to attend her aunt's funeral months before. I imagine she must have assumed so much time had passed, no one would care to dredge up the past again.

She was wrong.

Grace had kept tabs on Quinn's family over the years, waiting for the moment Quinn would slip up, and slip up she did.

Grace attended the funeral, slipping into a pew in the back without anyone knowing the real reason she was there. After it was over, she followed Quinn back home. Once she had her address, she did a little research and she discovered the woman was no longer going by the name of Brynn.

At first, all Grace was guilty of was a minor amount of stalking, and then she decided a little scare was in order. She broke into Quinn's home and left the lipstick message on her mirror. Grace thought that would be the end of it, until the rage she'd been carrying for so long gained a foothold in her heart. A new plan was formed, one that enticed Quinn to spend a week at the retreat.

As she prepared for Quinn's stay, the pain over the loss Grace had been suffering for so many years mounted. Lori had been taken from her, and it was time to take back, to make her pay for what she'd done. The night of Quinn's murder, she left the retreat, which we'd verified through surveillance video. She'd driven down the road about a half mile or so, returning on foot unnoticed when she came in through the back side of the property.

When asked why she moved Quinn's body after killing her, Grace's answer was a simple one. After she couldn't find the bullet or the shell casing, she thought Quinn had fallen on top of them, so she moved her.

Grace had taken Calvin's gun Sunday morning while he was at breakfast. A month earlier, the pair had a one-time dalliance, and when he'd gotten up to shower, Grace snooped around his place and found the gun in his nightstand drawer.

The plan was to kill Quinn and dispose of the gun, and she had the perfect hiding place for it—inside a hole in a hollowed-out tree on the property. At the time she was unaware Clara had seen her stash something inside the tree. Two days later, a curious Clara found the gun and confronted Grace. Caught off guard, Grace attempted to smooth things over, telling Clara she had no idea how the firearm came to be inside the tree. Clara's suspicions grew when Grace asked her to keep the gun's whereabouts quiet until she could speak to the police herself. Grace tried coming up with a way to spare Clara's life, but unless she sacrificed herself, there was none.

As for why she attacked my mother, she swore she meant her no real harm. She thought if she injured her, *just a little*, it might be enough to scare me off the case. It wasn't until she got to know me better that she realized fear tactics wouldn't work on me.

When asked about Quinn's journal, she admitted to taking it. She'd read through it and then burned it. And the cell phone? Tossed into a lake.

Another case closed.

As I sat on the back deck, watching the sun set over the ocean alongside Luka and Giovanni, I was struck with immense gratitude—for them and for the whole of my life, as crazy as it could be sometimes.

Giovanni gave my hand a squeeze and asked, "How does it feel to be home?"

"There's no place I'd rather be."

"You've earned yourself a well-deserved break after such a strenuous case. Why don't we take a vacation?"

I brushed my lips across his and said, "Sounds good to me."

As soon as the words were spoken, a curious feeling ran through me—a sense that while one case had closed, another was about to open.

THE END

Thank you for reading Little Shattered Dreams, book six in the *USA Today* bestselling Georgiana Germaine mystery series.

I hope you enjoyed getting to know the characters in this story as much as I have enjoyed writing them for you. This is a continuing series with more books coming before and after the one you just read. You can find the series order (as of the date of this printing) in the "Books by Cheryl Bradshaw" section below.

In Little Last Words, book seven in the series:

After living in a verbally abusive relationship for the past six years, twenty-seven-year-old Penelope Barlow has finally found the courage to leave. In the wee hours of night, she wakes her five-year-old daughter to play a game they've been practicing--getting to the car without waking Daddy.

The game is a success.

One month later, mother and daughter are enjoying their new beginning in Cambria, California, the same town where Penelope was raised. But someone in town isn't happy about her return. And for Penelope, her past is about to catch up to her present.

Want a sneak peek? Here's an exclusive look at chapter one …

LITTLE
LAST
WORDS

1

Penelope Barlow leaned back in the driver's seat, her thoughts drifting to the events that had taken place over last several weeks of her life. It had been almost a month since she'd moved back to the seaside town of Cambria, California. After spending the last six years in a verbally abusive relationship, she'd packed a couple of bags, waiting for the night she'd find the courage to leave Dean for good.

Courage came at long last when Dean accused Penelope of smiling at another man while they were out for dinner. After they returned home, he'd hit her for the first time, striking her so hard across the face it sent her hurdling onto the wall. She'd slumped to the ground, curling into a ball as he continued to deliver blow after blow.

In that moment, she'd realized it was time for the hell she'd been living through to be over.

She waited for Dean to fall asleep and then tiptoed her way to her five-year-old daughter's room to play a secret game they'd been practicing. The game was simple. All Sadie had to do was to follow Mommy out of the house without making a peep. If she made it inside Mommy's car without waking Daddy, Sadie would be rewarded with two scoops of ice cream the next day.

That night, mother and daughter fled toward a fresh start in a familiar town, the same town where Penelope had been raised. Family and friends welcomed them with open arms, ready and willing to offer their help and support.

Life was full of new beginnings in the tight-knit community, a town brimming with old memories.

Some memories were good, like the first kiss she'd had with Zachary Sandler at the Halloween dance in the ninth grade.

Some were bad, like the loss of her father years earlier.

There were other memories still, some she didn't like to think about.

As her thoughts returned to the present moment, Penelope peered into the rearview mirror and smiled. Sadie was fast asleep in her car seat, her head tipped to the side, her arms wrapped around a stuffed pink bunny, a gift from her grandmother. Staring at her daughter now, Penelope noticed how peaceful and content she seemed, a lot more content than the child had been in a long time.

Turning down the street toward home, Penelope rolled to a stop in front of a townhouse. It was the first place she'd ever rented on her own. At twenty-eight-years-old, it felt good to stand on her own two feet, providing a life for her and her daughter.

Penelope opened the driver's-side door, and Sadie's eyes popped open.

She yawned, rubbed her eyes, and said, "Mommy, I'm tired."

"I know, honey. Let's get you into your pajamas, and then you can go to bed."

Sadie shook her head. "I don't wanna go to bed yet."

Penelope laughed, unbuckled Sadie's car seat, and scooped her into her arms. "I'm sure you don't, but it's after your bedtime. Mommy's going to bed soon too."

"Can you read me a story first? Pleeeease?"

Penelope considered the request. "All right. A quick one."

"Oh…kay."

Half a story later, Sadie was fast asleep in her mother's arms. Penelope tucked her daughter into bed, gave her a kiss on the forehead, and went outside to get the groceries she'd left in the trunk of the car. She took the first load into the house and went back for the second. In the distance, a neighbor's dog began to bark. Soon after, the dog was joined by a second and then a third, until all the dogs in the neighborhood seemed to be barking in unison.

One last look around, Penelope grabbed the two remaining bags and brought them in. After the groceries were put away and a quick check on Sadie, Penelope crossed the hall into her bedroom. If there was one thing she needed right now, it was a shower. But when she stepped into the bathroom and flicked the light switch, the light didn't come on. It seemed odd—there were five bulbs in the light panel, and all of them had been working this morning.

How could all of them burn out on the same day?

Maybe they had, or maybe it was an electrical problem.

She checked her bedside lamps, the light in the closet, and the one on the balcony just off to the side of her room.

All the lights turned on, which made the situation even odder.

Penelope made a mental note to text the landlord in the morning and then grabbed a large, three-wick candle out of the hall closet. She set the candle on the bathroom counter, stripped off her clothes, and turned, watching the soft glow of the candle's flames cast flickers of shadows along the bathroom wall.

Pulling back the shower curtain, she froze.

Someone was behind the curtain, someone who uttered the last words Penelope would ever hear: "You didn't really think you'd get away with it. Did you?"

...

I hope you enjoyed the sneak peek!

Reserve your copy today on the
Cheryl Bradshaw Store at
CherylBradshawStore.com.

ABOUT CHERYL BRADSHAW

Cheryl Bradshaw is a New York Times and 11-time USA Today bestselling author writing in multiple genres, including mystery, thriller, romantic suspense, supernatural suspense, and poetry. She is a Shamus Award finalist for best private eye novel of the year, an eFestival of Words winner for best thriller, and has published over fifty books since 2011.

Raised in Southern California, she now lives in tropical Cairns, Australia, hiking in the rainforest, and diving in the Great Barrier Reef. When she's not writing, she loves to jet set to new countries, play with her sausage dog Luka, and eat her weight in cheese.

Sloane Monroe Series

Silent as the Grave (Prequel, Book 0)
When the body of Rebecca Barlow is found floating in the lake, private investigator Sloane Monroe takes on her very first homicide.

Black Diamond Death (Book 1)
Charlotte Halliwell has a secret. But before revealing it to her sister, she's found dead.

Murder in Mind (Book 2)
A woman is found murdered, the serial killer's trademark "S" carved into her wrist.

I Have a Secret (Book 3)
Doug Ward has been running from his past for twenty years. But after his fourth whisky of the night, he doesn't want to keep quiet, not anymore.

Stranger in Town (Book 4)
A frantic mother runs down the aisles, searching for her missing daughter. But little Olivia is already gone.

Bed of Bones (Book 5) (USA Today Bestselling Book)

Sometimes even the deepest, darkest secrets find their way to the surface.

Flirting with Danger (Book 5.5) A Sloane Monroe Short Story

A fancy hotel. A weekend getaway. For Sloane Monroe, rest has finally arrived, until the lights go out, a woman screams, and Sloane's nightmare begins.

Hush Now Baby (Book 6) (USA Today Bestselling Book)

Serena Westwood tiptoes to her baby's crib and looks inside, startled to find her newborn son is gone.

Dead of Night (Book 6.5) A Sloane Monroe Short Story

After her mother-in-law is fatally stabbed, Wren is seen fleeing with the bloody knife. Is Wren the killer, or is a dark, scandalous family secret to blame?

Gone Daddy Gone (Book 7) (USA Today Bestselling Book)

A man lurks behind Shelby in the park. Who is he? And why does he have a gun?

Smoke & Mirrors (Book 8) (USA Today Bestselling Book)

Grace Ashby wakes to the sound of a horrifying scream. She races down the hallway, finding her mother's lifeless body on the floor in a pool of blood. Her mother's boyfriend Hugh is hunched over her, but is Hugh really her mother's killer?

Sloane Monroe Stories: Deadly Sins

Deadly Sins: Sloth (Book 1)
Darryl has been shot, and a mysterious woman is sprawled out on the floor in his hallway. She's dead too. Who is she? And why have they both been murdered?

Deadly Sins: Wrath (Book 2)
Headlights flash through Maddie's car's back windshield, someone following close behind. When her car careens into a nearby tree, the chase comes to an end. But for Maddie, the end is just the beginning.

Deadly Sins: Lust (Book 3)
Marissa Calhoun sits alone on a beach-like swimming hole nestled on Australia's foreshore. Tonight, the lagoon is hers and hers alone. Or is it?

Deadly Sins: Greed (Book 4)
It was just another day for mob boss Giovanni Luciana until he took his car for a drive.

Deadly Sins: Envy (Book 5)
A cryptic message. A missing niece. And only twenty-four hours to pay.

Sloane & Maddie, Peril Awaits
(Co-Authored with Janet Fix)

The Silent Boy (Book 1)
In the hallway of a local tavern, six-year-old Louie Alvarez waits for his mother to take him home. A scream rips through the air, followed by the sound of a gun being fired. Louie freezes, then turns, with a single thought on his mind: RUN.

The Shadow Children (Book 2)

Within the tunnels of the historic port city of Savannah, fourteen-year-old Andi Leland has her mind set on freedom—not just for herself but for all the other teens who have come before her.

The Broken Soul (Book 3)

When the party of a lifetime becomes a party to the death, the lines become blurred. Friends become enemies. Drugs become weapons. And that's just the beginning.

The Widow Maker (Book 4)

A friend murdered. A business in trouble. A marriage struggling to survive. And that's just the beginning.

Georgiana Germaine Series

Little Girl Lost (Book 1)

For the past two years, former detective Georgiana "Gigi" Germaine has been living off the grid, until today, when she hears some disturbing news that shakes her.

Little Lost Secrets (Book 2)

When bones are discovered inside the walls during a home renovation, Georgiana uncovers a secret that's linked to her father's untimely death thirty years earlier.

Little Broken Things (Book 3)

Twenty-year-old Olivia Spencer sits at her desk in her mother's bookshop, dreaming about her upcoming wedding. The store may be closed, but she's not alone, and her dream is about to become her worst nightmare.

Little White Lies (Book 4)

When a serial killer sweeps through the streets of Cambria, California, Georgiana Germaine gets swept up into a tangled web of deception and lies.

Little Tangled Webs (Book 5)

What if you knew the person you loved was murdered, but no one else believed you? Eighteen-year-old Harper Ellis knows she's right, and she's prepared to risk her life to prove it.

Little Shattered Dreams (Book 6)

At fifty-five, Quinn Abernathy has been through her fair share of experiences in life. And tonight, her past is coming back to haunt her.

Little Last Words (Book 7)

After living in a verbally abusive relationship for the past six years, twenty-seven-year-old Penelope Barlow has finally found the courage to leave. But can she escape ... with her life?

Addison Lockhart Series

Grayson Manor Haunting (Book 1)

When Addison Lockhart inherits Grayson Manor after her mother's untimely death, she unlocks a secret that's been kept hidden for over fifty years.

Rosecliff Manor Haunting (Book 2)

Addison Lockhart jolts awake. The dream had seemed so real. Eleven-year-old twins Vivian and Grace were so full of life, but they couldn't be. They've been dead for over forty years.

Blackthorn Manor Haunting (Book 3)

Addison Lockhart leans over the manor's window, gasping when she feels a hand on her back. She grabs the windowsill to brace herself, but it's too late--she's already falling.

Belle Manor Haunting (Book 4)

A vehicle barrels through the stop sign, slamming into the car Addison Lockhart is inside before fleeing the scene. Who is the driver of the other car? And what secrets within the walls of Belle Manor will provide the answer?

Crawley Manor Haunting (Book 5)

Something evil is coming. Something dark. Something seeking to destroy everything and everyone in its path. And Addison Lockhart is the only one who can stop it.

Till Death do us Part Novella Series

Whispers of Murder (Book 1)

It was Isabelle Donnelly's wedding day, a moment in time that should have been the happiest in her life...until it ended in murder.

Echoes of Murder (Book 2)

When two women are found dead at the same wedding, medical examiner Reagan Davenport will stop at nothing to discover the identity of the killer.

Stand-Alone Novels

Eye for Revenge (USA Today Bestselling Book)

Quinn Montgomery wakes to find herself in the hospital. Her childhood best friend Evie is dead, and Evie's four-year-old son witnessed it all. Traumatized over what he saw, he hasn't spoken.

The Perfect Lie

When true-crime writer Alexandria Weston is found murdered on the last stop of her book tour, fellow writer Joss Jax steps in to investigate.

Hickory Dickory Dead (USA Today Bestselling Book)

Maisie Fezziwig wakes to a harrowing scream outside. Curious, she walks outside to investigate, and Maisie stumbles on a grisly murder that will change her life forever.

Roadkill (USA Today Bestselling Book)

Suburban housewife Juliette Granger has been living a secret life ... a life that's about to turn deadly for everyone she loves.